Jake threw his head back with a great gesture of impatience, half turning away but then spinning round to pin Emma with dark, irritated eyes.

'Look!' he snapped. 'People meet and fall in love at first glance, marry within days. I'm only asking you to pose for a picture. Do we have to exchange credentials and introductions for that? An artist grasps what he needs and right now I need you.'

Dear Reader

In this year of European unity, July sees the launch in hardback (September paperback) of an intriguing new series—contemporary romances by your favourite Mills & Boon authors, but with a distinctly European flavour. Look out for the special cover of a love story every month set in one of the twelve EC countries, which will take you on a fascinating journey to see the sights, life and romance, Continental style.

Vive l'amour in 1992—who do *you* think is Europe's sexiest hero?

The Editor

Patricia Wilson was born in Yorkshire and lived there until she married and had four children. She loves travelling and has lived in Singapore, Africa and Spain. She had always wanted to be a writer but a growing family and a career as a teacher left her with little time to pursue her interest. With the encouragement of her family she gave up teaching in order to concentrate on writing and her other interests of music and painting.

Recent titles by the same author:

INTANGIBLE DREAM
DEAREST TRAITOR
WALK UPON THE WIND

OUT OF NOWHERE

BY
PATRICIA WILSON

MILLS & BOON LIMITED
ETON HOUSE   18-24 PARADISE ROAD
RICHMOND   SURREY   TW9 1SR

*First published in Great Britain 1992
by Mills & Boon Limited*

© Patricia Wilson 1992

*Australian copyright 1992
Philippine copyright 1992
This edition 1992*

ISBN 0 263 77644 1

*Set in Times Roman 10 on 11¼ pt.
01-9208-56869 C*

Made and printed in Great Britain

CHAPTER ONE

THE fog that had been hanging around all the journey began to thicken as Emma left Exeter. It had been all right in the streets, under the lights where the shops were just closing and the pedestrians hurried along with their collars pulled well up, but it was somewhat different here. When the overhead lights had been left behind the road was just a murky ribbon of darkness, the headlights of the car only just penetrating the swirling mists.

It came uneasily to her mind that this was no sort of a place to break down, but she cheered herself up with the knowledge that only two days ago the car had been serviced. She had known what she was going to do, been perfectly well aware that she was about to run, although even that morning she had still told herself she could cope with everything.

What a lie! At the moment she didn't feel as if she could cope with anything at all. One more problem and she would simply shrivel up and fade into a mist too. This was more than a mist, Emma reminded herself. She felt it necessary to lean forward, to peer, to try and gain some more seeing distance, and it was all adding to a tension that had been growing for weeks.

Without her accident she could perhaps have managed. She had felt safe with Gareth, safer than she had felt with any man, and now she had to get away. It was still difficult to believe that he was married, and she could not look at things as he did. She could not shrug off the fact that he had a wife and family.

He had been angry when she had refused to see him any more and had told her quite plainly that he would not stop coming, never stop pressurising her. Flight had seemed the only way out, but with a bit more sense she would have set off earlier and stopped overnight if necessary. This was no sort of night to tackle Dartmoor.

A dark figure stepped into the road well in front of her and fingers of fear raced down her spine before she absorbed the fact that he was swinging a heavy torch, its light showing his companion in a dark blue uniform covered by a bright yellow jacket. The police! She slowed and stopped by them, pulling into the side of the road at their direction, and one of them came to lean in at the window she wound down.

'Are you alone, miss?'

'Yes. You can see that I——'

'How long are you going to be on the road?'

'I'm not quite sure. I think perhaps another half-hour, even less. I'm going to Credlestone Hall.' Emma was puzzled by their serious attitude. As far as she could tell, she hadn't done one unlawful thing.

'Credlestone Hall?' the policeman turned to his partner to enquire, his face caught in the light.

'It's on the moor itself. Isolated place. Eric Shaw lives there, as far as I remember.'

'He's my uncle,' Emma said. Now that she had company the tension had faded a bit and she almost laughed at the cunning of the man. He knew perfectly well who lived at the hall if he was from these parts and the deep burr of his voice told her he was. Eric Shaw was not only her uncle: he was famous.

'She's OK.'

She must have passed some small test because he was no longer looking at her as if she was a bank robber, and his companion took over again, leaning well in.

'No more stopping, then, miss,' he ordered firmly, 'and no picking up hitch-hikers. Got plenty of petrol, have you?'

'Yes,' Emma assured him breathlessly. She could see his partner walking round to the back of the car, looking in at the back seats, opening the boot she had never bothered to lock.

A torch was directed at her petrol gauge all the same, and she burst out uneasily, 'Look! What's happening? I suppose you know you're scaring me to death?'

'Prisoner on the loose from the Moor, that's all, miss. No need to worry, just keep going until you reach your uncle.'

No need to worry! Emma was so anxious that she clashed the gears as she moved off. Maybe she wouldn't have worried if it hadn't been so dark, so foggy, so murky. She felt a hysterical laugh coming on. Talk about one damned thing after another! Right at this moment she wished she had used some of her small savings and stayed overnight at Exeter. It would have been better to tackle Dartmoor in the light of day. Gareth had made her feel like a quarry and she was behaving like one.

The fog was now a grey blanket and she was peering so hard that her head began to ache. At any moment she expected to see some dark figure leap out from the hedge to stop her. And what if one did? Did she drive over him? It was all right those two telling her not to stop. She checked that the catches were down on every door and she gave her window one more twist to tighten it. Small precautions but all she could take.

There was absolutely nothing to see and her mind began to wander, travelling round and round as it had done for days, her thoughts back in the flat she had gladly left.

'It's not that I don't sympathise, Emma, but I honestly think you'll have to accept your uncle's offer.'

Sue Bright's face had been set in the lines of determination that Emma was beginning to recognise as the norm these days.

'I don't know Uncle Eric at all, really. He's always written to Daddy, but I've only actually met him once.'

'Well, does that matter? He did offer you a home, didn't he? And you now have no way of doing your job. Even if you only go for a while until you're—better... There's Gareth too. Honestly, you're pretty naïve not to know he was married. I can spot them a mile off. Anyway, he could easily keep you and I know perfectly well you're crazy about him. He must care about you too or he wouldn't still be chasing you now you're lame.'

'I'm not lame.'

Emma's sharp reply did nothing to soften the hard lines of Sue's face. When she had agreed to share this flat with Sue things had been different. She had been training at the hospital, her career as a physiotherapist all planned and straightforward. Sue was training too as a nurse and she had begged Emma to share the flat with her, to halve the rent and expenses. It had worked well until Sue's boyfriend had appeared on the scene.

Right from the first he had played up to Emma in a surreptitious way, all very humorous and cheerful but a look at the back of his eyes that was all too serious. It hadn't mattered too much at first when Gareth was her protection, and on the few occasions he had called to pick her up Roy Duncan had changed his tune considerably. Gareth was older, bigger and wealthy.

'I'll write and ask Uncle Eric again,' Emma offered. It wasn't such a bad idea, all things being considered.

It wasn't what Sue wanted.

'Can't you just go?' Her tight face tightened even more. 'It's not at the end of the universe. It's only Devon! What's to keep you here now? You're really lame since your accident,' she added with very deliberate cruelty. 'Anyway, Roy's thinking of moving in with me and you know you wouldn't like that. Neither would he. He finds you a bit stuffy and thinks you don't approve of two people living together.'

That was a real understatement. If he stayed here Emma wouldn't feel safe for one minute. Since her accident she had been more or less trapped here every time he came, and she dreaded the idea of his being here all the time.

'I suppose I could just go down there and take a chance,' she agreed quickly. 'I can manage quite well now. I have to see my consultant tomorrow but I could go down to Devon the next day if he approves.'

Why not? She had to get away from Gareth. He was nearly forty, old enough to be her father, as he had pointed out several times, but she could have married him, she was sure. He didn't frighten her as most men did. After her accident he had been wonderful, assuring her he would take care of her. It was only later that he had admitted he was already married, and it had been just one more blow.

This flat was the only nook and cranny she had in the world at the moment. It wouldn't be anything other than an additional problem if Roy Duncan moved in. He already knew she had stopped seeing Gareth. Sue had told him and he was worse than ever now with no thought of anyone stopping him.

'I'll go!' She made her mind up suddenly. One thing weighed against another, it was the only real escape she had. Uncle Eric's house was on Dartmoor, but it didn't have to be bleak and rainy. Even in late March there could be good weather, and she would be able to walk a little more each day. It would get her away from this situation. It would mean an escape from Gareth too.

The thought brightened her up a little. She had always wondered what Uncle Eric's house was like. He had come

to her father's funeral and it was the one and only time
she had seen him, but she had liked him instantly and
he had offered her a home whenever she chose to take
his advice and go down to him.

At that time she had been working at the hospital,
interested in her training, and the hard work had helped
her to cope with the loss of her father. It hadn't lasted
long. A few months later she had been knocked down
by a speeding car, and even after two operations and
weeks of pain her leg was still not better, the limp still
pronounced and the pain frequent.

Her money wouldn't last forever either. Soon she
would have to do some really serious thinking about hard
cash. They had never found the driver of the car, so
there had been no payment of compensation to ease
things over. Going to stay with Uncle Eric seemed to be
a good idea—if she could summon up the nerve. She
suddenly realised that Sue was staring at her hard, her
face beginning to lose its smile.

'It's a good idea. I'm glad you pushed me into it,'
Emma said cheerfully. 'It's given me something to think
about now. I'll get on with the planning tomorrow, di-
rectly after I've seen Mr Skelton.'

'I'll help you to pack when I come off duty tomorrow
afternoon,' Sue said, her smile back. 'Things are always
better when you've talked them over. Roy was only saying
last night that you're getting positively thin.'

It wasn't what Roy had said to her when Sue was out
of the room. Sue was right after all. She had to get out
of here.

When she went to the hospital Mr Skelton agreed that
a trip to Devon would be a good idea. Emma never told
him that actually it was Dartmoor. She knew him well.
When she had been training she had often worked on
his patients.

'Just remember, though, that we're not out of the wood by any means. You can walk now and things will improve all the time so long as you take gentle exercise and don't try anything foolish. We've got the scar down to a nice slim line now. We don't want any more operations. Are you still having a lot of pain?'

'Oh, no! It hardly bothers me now.'

It was a rather gallant lie and he knew it. The sort of injury she had faced and the type of operation left people in pain for a very long time. The knee was a very tricky place at the best of times. His smile was brief but there was admiration at the back of it.

'Go and enjoy yourself, then. I'll see you two weeks from today.'

It seemed to make everything all right and Emma's anxiety left her with a swift upward rush of hope as she said goodbye. She found herself looking forward to the move, her smile beginning to show. A smile that had been sadly lacking for months.

The smile was not there now. She drove through a village but the houses were almost invisible in the fog. It was only because she had planned her route carefully that she knew she was anywhere near her destination. She passed a sign, and reversed to have a closer look, hoping she could see without leaving the car.

She could—just. It said 'Credlestone'. This tiny village deep into the moors was the nearest thing to her uncle's house. Soon she would be there. She was shaken and stiff from the long drive but it would soon be over. The doubt at the back of her mind was pushed aside. Was it unforgivable to have come without warning? She had rushed to get away like a hunted creature and now nobody knew where she was, nobody expected her. If she had an accident nobody would even look for her.

She pulled herself up sharply and drove on, rubbing her aching leg and straining to see the twisting moorland road. She was out on the high moor. Even in daylight she knew it would be very isolated, and now it was frightening. She was cold, hungry and tired, praying the house would soon appear. From this point on she was simply guessing, but it must be close.

After weeks and weeks of inactivity and only careful exercise the journey here had taken more out of her than she had expected. She seemed to be right back to where she had been when she came out of hospital. Her left leg felt as if it were on fire, the strain of it making her head ache badly, and she longed to sit down with a hot drink.

The fog was thicker on the moor top, and there was a terrible loneliness about it. The whole landscape was alien, and Emma felt like an idiot who had walked deliberately into danger. She had been used to softer country all her life and later she had reluctantly grown accustomed to London. Even in the sunlight this place would be bleak and barren.

Her disgust at her own stupidity was growing by the second, but nothing really mattered if she could get to her uncle. He had looked too much like her father to let her down. She was very close to her destination and told herself firmly that everything would be all right.

It was not all right. She began to drive along a high narrow road, steep banks at either side, and, without warning, her lights failed. It was so unexpected that she didn't quite believe it. Braking was entirely automatic and luckily she was well in to the side of the road. She switched off the engine after several attempts to get the lights to work, and when she tried to switch on again there was no ignition at all.

She was stuck, alone, right out on the moor, and her mind went back to the two policemen and their reason for being out on this foggy night. She had no idea how to deal with a temperamental car and, even if she had known what to do, she dare not even think about stepping out into the foggy darkness. All she could do was sit there and pray for morning and help.

The cold deepened, making her leg ache worse. Sitting still was not improving matters, and she knew she should find her pain-killers and take two, but it wasn't easy to find them. There was absolutely no light and after a few frustrating minutes trying to feel around in her bag in the darkness she decided to give up. She would just have to stick it out.

Light came then, dazzling light that filled the car, all the more brilliant because it was so unexpected. It took a second to realise it was the glare of headlights and that she had heard the sound of a car. If she hadn't been so frustrated, so concerned about her leg, she would have been alert to the danger of a car coming behind her at speed on this narrow road.

Emma heard the scream of brakes being applied and for one brief minute she felt overwhelmed with relief. She was no longer alone. Whoever it was, she knew they would help. The euphoria lasted long enough for her to reach for the door catch in an attempt to gain assistance. Reasoning came swiftly and just in time. She remembered the police. She remembered where she was. How did she know that the man they were seeking had not stolen a car?

She pushed the lock quickly back into place and sat as she had done before, cold, aching and perfectly still. It was a bit stupid, she knew. After all, she needed help, but she had learned very early in life that self-preservation was the most important thing to consider always. Her father had taught her that and he had taught her well.

There was the sound of a car door being slammed and firm steps coming forward. She was still bathed in the light from the other car but she didn't turn round. When a dark face looked in at her she just stared back, determined not to be coaxed out of her small area of security, and any concerned looks he was giving her faded as she stared at him blankly.

'Why the hell are you parked here with no lights? Who were you trying to kill, yourself or me?'

He wasn't at all gentle and she could hear him very well because he was annoyed enough to raise his voice. All the energy seemed to have drained out of her, taking her voice with it, and she just stared back at him through the window.

He gave a sharp rap on the glass. 'Open the window!'

Emma's teeth sank into her bottom lip as she looked at him, considering what to do. If he was all right then she needed help and certainly didn't want to antagonise him further. If he was the man on the run she had better not make any sort of move to open either the window or the door. He could see her perfectly well, she assumed, but she couldn't see him beyond a tall, powerful outline. Suppose he broke the glass? What action should she take then? She had absolutely no weapon to hand.

'Open the window!' He raised his voice further to an actual roar, and she wound the window down just a tiny crack, reckoning he couldn't even get his fingers in that.

'What do you want?' Her voice was husky with cold and she seemed to have taken his breath away for a second. He bent further and peered through the minute gap.

'What do I *want* . . .?' He gave a sort of angry growl. 'Lady, I want to know why you're sitting here as if it were a summer afternoon. I want to know why you're blocking the road at the narrowest part, right on a blind bend. I want to know where your lights are. I wouldn't mind seeing a certificate of mental health!'

'I haven't got any.'

'I believe you!'

'L-lights...I mean.'

She heard his breath hiss out between clenched teeth, and he rattled the door-handle.

'OK. Open up.'

He straightened up, expecting instant obedience, and she could see how big he was, how really tall. She wouldn't stand a chance against a man like that. Even if she could have run there was as yet no place to run to.

She wound the window down just a little more with great caution. Making her voice very firm to show him she was no easy victim, she said, 'I'm sorry, but I really can't do that. After all, I don't know you.'

He bent again and peered in at her. She could feel his attitude. It was bristling with rage, but she had to consider her own safety. She could see his eyes now. They looked very dark but it might have been just that the fog was thick and the blackness total outside the range of the blazing headlights of his car.

'*What* did you say?'

'I said I can't open the door,' she repeated clearly. 'It's dark, miles from anywhere, and you must understand how I feel. I don't know you.'

'Of course you do,' he snarled. 'I'm the man you damn near killed. I'm the one with good brakes. Open the blasted door!'

He looked as if he was strong enough to take the door off its hinges, and he wasn't trying to hide or he would have put his own lights out. Emma made a rapid calculation of her chances and reluctantly released the catch.

'Move over!'

Suddenly he was getting into the car, and she almost shot into the passenger-seat, hurting her knee and not quite stifling the moan of pain. It sounded like panic, she could even hear that herself, and it earned her a disgusted look.

'Slipped your keeper, did you?' he rasped sarcastically, manoeuvring himself into the driving-seat. It wasn't easy. She was driving a Mini and the man was big and powerful, broad-shouldered. He had dark hair and he looked most forbidding. She didn't answer because it seemed to be the best course of action.

He tried the ignition and got no response. Emma wanted to tell him she'd tried that, but she didn't fancy another explosion of rage and she had enough to do keeping a wary eye on him.

He bent and released the catch for the bonnet and then got out and went to his own car. He was back in a second with a torch and after one look under the bonnet he gave a disgruntled mutter and slammed it down, coming back to the open door.

'Burnt-out wires,' he snapped. 'Heaven knows how it moved at all.'

'But I've just had it serviced,' Emma informed him crossly. It merely gained her a sceptical look.

'Your keeper did it? No wonder you gave him the slip. All right, where are you going?'

She was beginning to get thoroughly annoyed at his attitude in spite of her fear, and Emma gained enough courage to glare at him.

'I'm going to Credlestone Hall,' she snapped. 'In fact, I must be almost there.'

For a second he seemed to stiffen and then he crouched down, looking in at her, really noticing her for the first time, his anger somewhat subdued.

'You are. Two more bends and the house is visible—in normal circumstances. Well, there's no way you're going to get there unless I take you. In any case, this car can't be left here. There's not much traffic on this road and nobody is going to expect to find a car without lights blocking the way. If I don't move you there'll be an accident.'

'You were going fast,' Emma said irritably. It earned her another of those disgusted looks.

'Be thankful I wasn't either a tractor or a tank. Get back behind the wheel.'

He slammed the door and she struggled across. He was rude, she decided, rude and unpleasant. He wasn't an escaped convict, though, because he was well dressed, as far as she could see. His leather jacket looked very well cut. She had another chance to look at it as he came from his car with a rope and proceeded to kneel down and tie it to the front of her car. Yes, he looked quite well-off. And he was horrid!

He drove round in front of her and then came back to speak.

'I'm going to tow you. Take the handbrake off, put the car in neutral and steer; follow my lights.'

Brisk, to the point and rude, she mused. He hadn't even waited for her to nod her agreement. Her leg was hurting so much now that she could have screamed, and she wouldn't have minded screaming at him but she would soon be at Credlestone Hall with her uncle and this bad tempered man would be on his way.

She felt the car begin to move and she steered very, very carefully. If she did one thing wrong he would probably get out and shake her. He seemed to think he could say anything he liked to her as it was. The sooner she saw the back of him, the better. There was one good thing. She had finally been too annoyed with him to be scared that he was a man.

She hoped her uncle wouldn't mind about this. It was over a year since her uncle had offered to have her at

Credlestone Hall. Maybe he hadn't meant it? It was, after all, the sort of thing he would have felt impelled to say at a time like that, knowing as he did that there were no other relatives. Maybe he had forgotten? She should not have let things drive her away so precipitously. She should have stayed longer and written to Uncle Eric.

It all seemed a bit childish now, and through her long time in hospital after her accident she had not written to him. Later she had been afraid he would think she was filled with self-pity. Suppose he didn't want her here? She would be a very awkward addition to his household, especially in her present state of health.

Suddenly she saw the house, tall and forbidding, as grey as the fog that surrounded it. It loomed out of the wreaths of wet mist as if it carried its own atmosphere and climate. For a second the fog swirled away, giving her the first glimpse of her uncle's home.

It stood on a slight rise with a few trees in what seemed to be a large garden. A path led to the front, a wooden gate and a rough stone wall its only defence against the lonely road. It could not have stood in a more forsaken place or looked less welcoming.

Credlestone Hall! Whatever she had been expecting, it was certainly not this secret and isolated house. It took away any feeling she had nursed of warmth and welcome. She felt like a stranger coming to a strange place.

Emma thought she could see a chink of light from one of the windows. There were probably thick curtains. Somebody had to be there because she couldn't go any further and she knew it, whatever her welcome. She was on the verge of collapse and she knew she had pushed herself too much, come too far.

He seemed to be towing her past the house and her hand hit the horn, but there was no horn either and she was glad there had not been when she found he was merely towing her round the back. Her uncle would hear them and come out to deal with this dark, angry stranger and she would be in the lights and quite safe, even if he was startled to see her. Everything could be reviewed tomorrow.

Nobody appeared as they stopped and Emma got out into the wet fog, instantly chilled as she began the struggle to drag her cases from the back seat of the car. It was a long way up to the house but there was no way she was asking this man for further help. Now that the noise of the car had stopped the silence seemed to rush forward and surround her like the fog and gathering night, and her temper at the man's attitude was somewhat quenched when she thought of his size.

There were no lights at all round the back and she had the truly dreadful feeling that she was stranded here, facing an empty house. Why didn't her uncle come? Surely he had heard the car's engine, surely somebody had? She was almost positive she had seen a chink of light from the front.

She lifted her cases, realising how heavy they were after only a few hesitant steps. Her leg was now excruciatingly painful and the path was stony, making walking difficult, the stones cutting into the soles of her fashionable shoes. This was a path for hiking boots, not soft red leather.

She felt utterly isolated and vulnerable very quickly. The fog drowned all sound and she wanted to get inside as fast as possible. When she was in the light, her uncle beside her, she would thank this dark giant, this frightening rescuer, and he would go.

She began to hurry, stumbling over the stones, the fog wetting her long hair. Memory of a long time ago tried to surface but she squashed it hurriedly. It would be all right. Uncle Eric was like her father, dependable, safe— like Mr Skelton. Nothing could happen to her.

'You little fool! Give me those!' A hard hand jerked her to a stop and her dark rescuer almost snatched the cases from her.

'I—I can manage, thank you.'

'The hell you can! Go on ahead and open the door.'

He thought she lived here! He thought it was her house, her home. She must get him to go away before she met her uncle. She didn't want him standing there while she explained her sudden decision to flee London. Maybe the door was open? Maybe she could just step inside, thank him and then wait for him to go? She would tell him to put the cases on the step.

The door swung open as she tried the knob but he didn't give her time to say anything. He simply stepped into the house beside her, looking down at her in the gloom, an air of menace about him that she could not mistake.

It terrified her, and she didn't care now what he knew or what he heard, she just shouted out, 'I'm here! It's Emma! I'm so relieved to get here. This man helped because I...!' His quick low laugh made shivers run down her back, and his words added to her growing fear.

'You really are deranged, aren't you? Quite bizarre. What are you doing, practising for a part in a play?'

Her own voice seemed to have choked up and she again noticed his height, the width of his shoulders.

'I'm letting him know I'm here.' She couldn't manage a real voice. The sound was almost a whisper.

'There's absolutely nobody in the house but the two of us.' The quiet of his voice sounded threateningly satisfied, and Emma moved back against the wall, her attitude defensive. She would fight! She wouldn't let this just happen.

'You're lying! I saw a light.' She suddenly had a terrible thought. 'Where is this place? You haven't brought me to Credlestone Hall!'

'Indeed I have,' he said quietly.

'Then thank you for your help. I can manage now.' Emma was shaking but she knew she had to gain some mental supremacy. 'My uncle lives here.'

'No. *I* live here.'

'Oh, no, you don't, not if this is Credlestone Hall! Who are you?' She made her shaking voice sharp, knowing she must keep the advantage.

'More to the point, I think, who are you? I think the time has come to find out all about you.'

The voice was as dark as the night, and Emma realised she was standing in a silent house with a man who was a complete stranger, a man who stood perfectly still and watched her from the shadows.

Pictures she had long ago suppressed flashed into her mind, bringing her out in a cold sweat. Pain in her leg was growing to an unbearable crescendo and she panicked, spinning round to run, knowing perfectly well that it was madness but utterly incapable of being sane.

The step was wet and slippery and she lost her footing immediately; her leg almost locked, as stiff as wood. She threw her arms out to save herself, knowing that a blow would damage her knee even more, and an arm lashed around her waist, lifting her and bringing her into the hall, out of the wet fog.

'Don't! Please!' She was quite mindless with fear now, all she had been carefully taught forgotten as he held her against the power of his chest. He reached out and flicked on a light, still holding her as he looked down into her frantic eyes.

'Please!' she sobbed, and she saw his face then, dark, sardonic and utterly exasperated.

'A mad thing from the moor,' he muttered. 'Well, at least it makes you interesting.'

Dark eyes stared at her and he swung her completely up into his arms as he turned away from the door, his dark eyebrows raised in annoyance when she plucked uselessly at his arm.

'Save it!' he rasped irritably. 'Now that I've captured you, I'll have a look at you; escape is unlikely, so save your strength. If you succeeded in making a break for it I'd catch you in seconds. You owe me an explanation, my girl.'

Emma didn't know what he meant, but he was a man and he was strong. Her heart was hammering frantically, and suddenly violent pain shot up her leg from the knee, the final blow after a nightmare journey and its terrifying end. She fainted.

CHAPTER TWO

WHEN Emma opened her eyes she nearly closed them again in fright. Other eyes were watching her, dark eyes, deeply brown. She was lying on a comfortable settee in front of a roaring fire, the room softly lamplit around her, and the man was crouching by her side.

He was very close to her, watching her intently, his face lean and dark, black eyebrows drawn together in a scowl. It was a handsome face but an unusual one, a sort of fine-drawn irritability in the well-cut features. He was tanned, but there was an olive tint under the skin as if he would never be actually pale. His hair was dark too, almost as dark as her own, and slightly long, just flecked here and there with silvery threads, although he couldn't have been much more than thirty-four or -five. He said nothing at all, no word of comfort or reassurance; all he did was watch her, and all her fear came pouring back.

She stiffened, drawing further away, her eyes wide open, and a wave of exasperation flashed across his face.

'Isn't this where you expected to be?' he asked ironically. 'If you'd care to faint again I could arrange you in a different position for your return to life. We've got beds, or I could just stand and hold you. You don't weigh a great deal.'

There was a speculation in his voice that wasn't exactly amusement, and she made a quick move to get up and away from him.

'Don't start again!' he warned sharply. 'For the moment you're fairly well penned. To escape you'd have

23

to fight your way past me, make it to the door and race down the path to a useless car. All or any of those things are just not possible, so forget it. I'd have you back here in two shakes.'

A sick feeling bubbled up inside her. The house was isolated, the door shut, empty miles of moorland around them. It was perfectly obvious that her uncle wasn't here or he would have been right beside her now. Perhaps this wasn't Credlestone Hall. Perhaps this man had lied to get her in here. Or perhaps it was and he had broken in when he knew Uncle Eric was away.

'Why—why do you want me here?' Emma asked shakily. 'You won't get away with this.'

She felt she shouldn't really be quite so scared. The room was warm and inviting, and the man hadn't done anything to her yet. No amount of logic helped, though. Fear was too deeply rooted in her past; there were too many memories now right at the top of her mind.

'Get away with it? Well, I expect to be punished for my crimes. It might help if you could tell me what they are. As to wanting you here, I don't want you here at all. I just want to know who the hell you are.'

He stared at her intently, his dark eyes narrowed as he noted her slenderness, the length of hair still damp and the widened deep blue eyes that seemed to fill her pale face. He seemed to be angrily examining every feature, and all she could do was stare back. She dared not make a move now, not after his quick and annoyed reaction to her previous attempt to get up.

'Are you going to enlighten me?' he muttered irritably, his dark eyebrows raised. 'If you plan to stay there staring at me I'd better get more comfortable. Take your time; we have all night at the very least.'

'What do you mean?' Emma watched him closely too because it was possible that if she took her eyes off him he would make some irreversible move, and she was as much on guard as a wary cat.

'Look! You're stuck here, or, to put it impolitely, I'm stuck with you. You have a car that can't be moved, the fog is thick and almost impassible, you look cold, hungry and fairly wild. Why I should be at the receiving end of your suspicions quite astounds me. I brought you to your destination, luggage included,' he reminded her acidly. 'You were either expecting to arrive here for some good reason or you're an escaped lunatic with two suitcases.'

Colour came flooding into her cheeks, her anxiety momentarily doused by annoyance.

'I'm wondering if you're the lunatic. You haven't done much to set my mind at rest, have you?'

Her blue eyes flashed and he just watched her face, his eyes on her flushed cheeks. His silence sent a strange wave of awareness through her skin that worried her, and she grew cooler still. Hauteur was a good defence.

'I'd like to sit up,' she said coldly. 'You're the one with explanations to make, because if this is Credlestone Hall it's my uncle's house and you've no business to be here.'

'Sit up by all means.' He gave her a mocking look and drew back only far enough to give her room to get her legs down. The movement was painful and she bit into her lips, longing to ask for a drink so she could take her tablets, but determined not to make one false move.

He just went on staring at her. Clearly he was not about to explain his presence here and she got nervous all over again, but there was something about him that was also infuriating.

'You're trying to frighten me!' Emma forced herself to sit up straighter, even though her head was swimming. 'You tried your best to frighten me at the door.'

'I succeeded,' he remarked smoothly.

'You merely shocked me, standing there so silently. *And* it was deliberate!'

He frowned rather alarmingly. 'Let's compare shocks, shall we?' he suggested irritably, his rather brooding looks fading. 'I discover you huddled in a car, making no move to even flash a torch. Upon your arrival here you hurtle towards the house and then start calling to a non-existent person. You then try to race away to God knows where, faint, and return to consciousness, demanding explanations from *me*. All that may be normal in your world; in mine it's decidedly odd.'

He looked as if he would seriously consider putting her through the front door and locking it behind her, and she was as scared of the dark, wild moor as she was of him—more scared.

'My name is Emma Shaw. You said this was Credlestone Hall, so it must be my Uncle Eric's house. You know perfectly well I was calling out because I expected to find him here.' She suddenly realised he looked quite at home in this house. 'I suppose you might be some sort of strange guest. Where is my uncle?'

Instead of answering, he stood slowly and stared down at her. If anything his face had tightened even more. Her credentials certainly didn't please him.

'Eric is in America,' he said with a narrow-eyed look at her that spoke volumes. 'I said I live here and so I do, temporarily.'

'Oh! How—how temporarily?' The bit of confidence she had managed to gain by facing him began to ebb away. If Uncle Eric had let his house to this man then where was she going to go, and how was she going to go anywhere when her car was broken down?

'One whole year, starting last month,' he said decisively.

A year! What on earth was she going to do? He just stood looking down at her and it reminded her rather forcefully that this was a tall, powerful man and that the rest of the house was silent. They were all alone. Her hands went nervously to the buttons of her dress, checking that she was still reasonably intact, and the black eyebrows scowled in irritation.

'Naturally, I'll go!' she said quickly. 'I had no idea that Uncle Eric had let the house.'

'He hasn't. We don't let houses to each other in our sphere, we lend them.' He made her sound either mercenary or stupid, she couldn't decide which.

'Yes—well—anyway, I'll—I'll go.'

'You'll walk to the village in the thick fog, carrying your suitcases and wait for tomorrow's bus to take you to tomorrow's train, I assume?' he asked with cutting sarcasm. 'If you're Eric's niece then naturally you'll stay here.'

'I don't want to, thank you.' She managed to stand without swaying. 'If you've taken the house for a year then clearly I'm not going to intrude further. Obviously I should have written or telephoned.'

'And why didn't you?'

His soft question had her face flushing again and she looked away quickly. 'It was a sort of spur-of-the-moment decision. He—he invited me last year when my father died and...'

'And you're in some sort of a fix, so you decided to take him up on his offer really fast—over a year later.'

'It's none of your business!' Emma stated sharply, looking round for her bag and wondering how she was going to get out of the door without giving her lameness away. If he knew she was lame he would have a sort of hold on her. Not that she knew what she was going to do when she got outside.

'What are you so scared of,' he asked softly, 'apart from men, of course?'

He was leaning against the mantelpiece, his hands in his pockets, and he looked completely overpowering.

'I'm not scared at all.'

She decided that enough was enough and moved, but her leg had other plans; it let her down, and she fell back to the settee with a low murmur, the depth of pain forcing tears to her eyes.

'You hurt yourself on that step?' He was back beside her at once, his face annoyed. 'Why the hell didn't you tell me instead of sitting there, exchanging delirious banter?'

'I didn't! It wasn't!' she began heatedly. 'You brought it on. You wanted to know about... Don't touch me!' she gasped as his hand came to her leg.

'My, my, you *do* have a hang-up about men, don't you?' He stood again, looking at her intently. 'Let's get some sense into this mad situation. You say you're Emma Shaw and I expect you are. Your uncle owns this house and lent it to me for a year. I don't want you here, but as you're Eric's niece I can't see any alternative but to have you here for the time being. You can stay here a couple of days until I decide what to do about you. I don't imagine Eric will take too kindly to it if I throw you out into the fog. Assuming he actually did offer to have you here.'

He looked at her derisively, clearly not believing her, and she had not the slightest doubt that he didn't want her here at all. It made her feel safe for now, anyway. He would want to keep as far from her as she wanted to keep from him, *if* he was telling the truth!

'How do I know that...?' she began uneasily, clinging on to her suspicions like a fetish.

'You just have to live through the night,' he grated. 'In the morning Eric's housekeeper comes from the village. She doesn't live in but she's been here a long time. If you're genuine I expect she'll know all about you. If you're not genuine I can always toss you out tomorrow.'

He shot her a look of dislike and it had her apologising for some reason, 'I—I'm sorry. I'll stay, of course.'

'I was afraid you'd say that,' he murmured caustically. 'I'll take your cases up, show you your room and then we'll eat.' She just sat there, not wanting him to see her move, and he looked round, his mouth in a tight line. 'Obviously I've said the wrong thing again. You do eat, don't you?'

'Yes—er—yes. I'll help.'

'No need. Mrs Teal leaves me well supplied. I can manage to serve two.'

Well, he certainly didn't want her here. That was good. She waited until he walked out with her cases and then stood again, carefully flexing her leg and managing to follow him slowly. Her head was pounding, her leg was hurting badly and she didn't want the humiliation of a sardonic stranger seeing her like that. Let him get started upstairs and she would follow.

As a subterfuge it was a failure. He was waiting in the hall, his eyes on her uneven movements as she came out into the relative gloom. He put the cases down and flicked the lights on.

'Why are you being so damned stubborn?' he rasped. 'You hurt yourself. What have you done, twisted a muscle?'

'Er—yes,' Emma assured him hastily, grasping the chance to cover up. 'I expect it will be all right tomorrow.'

'Want some help upstairs?' He sounded a little more kind, but she shook her head quickly. He now looked taller than ever, his physical appearance completely dominating. He had a black polo-neck sweater on and dark jeans; added to his quite dark face, it made him look sinister—devilish. His eyes were funny too, deepset, dark, resentful and very watchful.

'No, thank you. I'm used to managing.'

Her face flushed at this major slip but he simply shrugged and picked up the cases again, walking ahead.

'Twist your leg regularly, do you?' he enquired scathingly over his shoulder. 'It must be all the escape attempts you have to go through.'

She decided to keep quiet, following him slowly upstairs, her eyes anxiously on his broad shoulders, and he said nothing else at all, flinging a door open and showing her into a lovely old bedroom that sprang into view as he switched on the lights.

'Here's your room. The sheets and other things are in the cupboard at the end of the passage. Better make your bed up while I dish out the meal. You look about fit to drop down. Don't be too long either—the food won't keep hot and I'm too hungry to wait.'

He stood looking at her for a minute, his dark face almost satanic, his eyes piercingly intent, and she shivered. That irritated masculinity seemed to be just on the edge of violence, and who was there to bear the brunt of any violence but herself? Even though this was her uncle's house, he was leaving her in no doubt at all that she was intruding.

He suddenly walked out, closing the door hard, and Emma sat on the bed to rest a while. The stairs had almost finished her off. This was a situation she had not envisaged, and this man would probably throw her out tomorrow. Then what would she do? Maybe her uncle would be back in a few days? The fact that he had someone living here wouldn't be a bar to that if they were friends. The thought cheered her and she got slowly to her feet to go along the passage and collect the bedding she needed, trying to ignore the pain in her leg and the pounding headache.

She kept seeing the dark face in her mind, wondering about him. She had never liked young men of her own age, and she sometimes wondered if it came from being so close to her father after her mother's death.

Her father had brought her up almost single-handed and still held down a very responsible job; nobody in his parish was neglected because he was a widower with a small daughter. Being the vicar of St Jude's hadn't left him with much money, and it had not left Emma with a home after he had died. To her, though, he had been the most wonderful of men and he was too hard an act to follow. Gareth had seemed to be the same, but he had shown his true colours in the end.

This man was frightening in an entirely different way from any other. He was secret, powerful, strange. Gareth hadn't been like that. He was the only man apart from her father she had ever felt comfortable with. He had treated her carefully, made her feel normal and safe. This man made her feel angry and that was unusual in itself.

He called her before she had even done more than put the bedding down on the bed, and there was nothing in his voice that gave encouragement.

'Miss Shaw?' He was obviously standing at the bottom of the stairs. 'I've served the meal. Come down now.'

It annoyed her all over again. His tone was irritated even when he was calling her to a meal. He had also suggested that she was a little odd. Odd! He was all of that, with his dark face and his scowls. She went out and was thankful he was no longer standing there to see her try to manage the stairs. She made it down safely and followed the delicious smell to the kitchen just in time to see him putting the meal on the pine table.

'I gave up the idea of dining in any sort of splendour tonight,' he said briefly, glancing up at her. 'Tomorrow no doubt you'll want to explore the house, and you'll discover the dining-room I rarely use. Tonight we'll eat here.'

She was a bit surprised when he came round and politely held her chair for her; still, he wasn't in any way an uncouth man, it was just that he was cold and sardonic, besides being unwelcoming and utterly frightening.

He had a lovely voice but his frequent scowls were quite off-putting. Not that she wanted to be friendly with him. She was glad he didn't like her. It gave her a measure of security.

She suddenly found his dark eyes observing her and she got the flustered feeling that he had been reading her mind.

'Mrs Teal left a casserole. I warmed it up. Luckily she leaves plenty, so your unexpected arrival doesn't really matter.'

He looked away and began to eat, and Emma struggled to find something to say. She didn't want to go on fighting because she wasn't up to it and, in any case, she had to stay a while somehow.

'I—I don't know your name,' she began hopefully, but he glanced quickly up and then looked away again.

'Jake.' Apparently that was the end of the conversation.

'Don't you have another name?'

He glanced up again at her hesitant voice, his dark brows drawn together as usual. 'Does it matter?'

'Well, as we're both in the same house——'

'Not by any choice of mine and not for long,' he bit out coldly, adding in a very grudging tone, 'Garrani. Jake Garrani.'

It took a minute to settle, and then she gasped, gazing at him in fascination.

'The painter? *That* Garrani?'

'*That* Garrani!' he agreed acidly. 'You're a connoisseur of fine art, Miss Shaw?'

'No, I'm not!' Her face flushed at his insulting tone and she sat very straight. 'I just happened to see an item on television about you. It was when that painting was being auctioned, *Ecstasy*.'

She stopped suddenly and looked down at her meal, beginning to eat hastily. The picture had been absolutely beautiful but a bit erotic. Whoever the model had been, she was the most beautiful woman Emma had ever seen. There had been some talk as to why he had sold it. He didn't need the money, although it had fetched thousands.

Apparently he made a fortune painting portraits of the famous. They had to wait in strict order to get in with him, and he didn't beat about the bush if he had something to say to them. Not that *Ecstasy* had been what she would have called a portrait. It had been an astonishing nude—brilliant, but...

Who he was explained his rudeness to her, though. If he showed veiled contempt for foreign princesses he wasn't going to be too careful with Emma Shaw. But it didn't altogether explain his friendship with her uncle. Her uncle was an artist, but he was an illustrator. His illustrations of animals were quite famous. Any good nature book had his fine line drawings and coloured impressions of animals of all sorts. She didn't know if it came under the heading of fine art but she doubted it.

Jake Garrani was a giant in the art world. What was he doing down here? They had said on television that he had studios in New York and in Italy. His father had been an Italian, which explained the name and the rather dark good looks. It didn't explain the glowering attitude—Italians were supposed to be sunny people. It didn't explain how he could be friendly with Uncle Eric either. Her uncle had seemed to her to be exactly like her father, quiet and kind. It made her suspicious all over again.

'When is my uncle due back, Mr Garrani?' she asked carefully.

'The name is Jake, and I'd be very obliged if you'd stick to that during your brief sojourn,' he grated, adding irritatedly, 'Eric is in America at the moment, and he leaves for Africa next month, as far as I can remember.'

'Africa!' She felt a wave of sheer dismay. He wasn't coming back, then? What was she to do?

'What's so strange about Africa? He paints animals. He's been commissioned to do a book about the cheetah.' He looked at her derisively, as if she were an impostor. 'Or didn't you know he was a respected illustrator?'

'Of course I know!' She glared at him and for a moment their eyes held. He was the one who looked away first. Apparently there was something about her that irritated him beyond the normal.

'I had wondered if you merely decided to own him when you had trouble,' he murmured scathingly, 'or even if you own him at all. Obviously you've never been here before. Even now you keep asking yourself if this is Credlestone Hall or if I've brought you here out of the fog for some murky reason of my own. Just don't have any further flights of fancy and start calling me Uncle Eric. He's sixty-five and short and round as a barrel. I'm six foot two.'

'I know perfectly well what my uncle looks like!'

His words had hit a bit close to the mark and she struggled to her feet, determined to storm off.

'Sit down and eat!' His lean brown hand shot across the table and captured her wrist, his fingers frighteningly strong. He looked up at her darkly. 'I'm sorry. I have no right to speak to you like that. It's none of my business. Let's just say that you've caught me at a bad time.'

If he thought that was an excuse Emma didn't, but, short of an undignified struggle, she could think of no way of simply walking off. She sat down.

'Do—do you think I could have a glass of water?' she asked in a low voice, ignoring his rough apology.

'Don't you drink wine, or are you too scared to notice I've poured you a glass?'

'I noticed, thank you,' she muttered. 'I'm not at all scared. I—I have to take a tablet, though.'

He got up without another word and fetched her a drink, but as her hand came out of her handbag with the tablets his fingers closed again over her wrist.

'What are they?' He sounded sharp and suspicious, as if she were a drug addict, and she looked up at him resentfully.

'I have a bad headache!'

He took the bottle anyway and read it with a frown.

'Pretty strong tablets for a headache. Where did you get these?'

'The doctor. Are you a pharmacist as well as an artist, Mr Garrani?' She was being as sarcastic as he had been, and he didn't even bother to answer. What he did do, however, was move her wine away as if she would have been stupid enough to drink anything at all except tea or water with strong pain-killers.

'I would like to point out that I'm not a child!' Emma snapped.

'I'm not treating you as a child. I'm just making sure I don't have a body on my hands.'

He never even looked up. He was perfectly horrid. She glared at him but it only made her headache worse, and as he wasn't looking it was pointless anyway. She prepared to eat her meal in silence, determined not to speak to him again at all.

After the meal, to her surprise, he made coffee and she found herself being urged back into the warm firelight and lamplight of the room she had first seen as he carried a tray in and advised her to follow. She did. She had quite finished with arguments for the day. All she wanted now was a warm bath for her stiff and painful leg and a long sleep.

'Black or white?' He sat by the coffee-table and looked up.

'White, please.' She was astonished at this politeness, and it was pretty ridiculous, sitting here with a man she disliked and who wanted her out with great speed. It was silly to go on being scared too. Her panic was subsiding. 'I—I expect you came here to work?' she ventured when she found that silence was an uncomfortable thing, but there seemed to be no topic of conversation that could interest him.

'No,' he said flatly, coming across and handing her the coffee before moving back to his chair. 'I'm thinking about working, but that's not why I came here at all.' He looked up sharply, his dark eyes direct. 'We're both on the run, Miss Shaw.'

'I'm not... What are you on the run from, Mr Garrani?'

'Jake!' he corrected acidly. 'I'm running from too much commercial work for one thing; the other thing is—private.'

'I'm sorry. I wasn't meaning to pry. You did bring the subject up.'

'Did I, Miss Shaw?' He looked at her steadily over the rim of his cup. 'Perhaps it's because you seem determined to speak to me.'

Emma stirred restlessly, uncomfortable with those dark, intent eyes on her. She had read somewhere that Italians had liquid eyes. There was nothing liquid about these eyes. They were like polished black marble. It should have been a relief to be disliked by a man like this but, oddly enough, it irked.

'It doesn't matter, I'll be leaving tomorrow,' she said quickly.

'What a splendid idea. Where will you run? Back to the vicarage?'

It banished any nervousness on Emma's part because it did prove that he knew her uncle. He couldn't have got the information from anywhere else, unless he was simply being sarcastic about her appearance. She stood up, furious at his hard cruelty.

'You may be famous and talented, Mr Garrani,' she blazed, 'but you're possibly the rudest, nastiest man I've ever met!'

'You'll soon get used to it,' he assured her drily. 'After a good night's sleep you'll have recovered sufficiently to ignore me.'

'I should think that most people ignore you when they can,' Emma retorted. 'You must be a very lonely man.'

'And you?' he enquired softly. 'Where are your friends, Miss Shaw? I know what I'm running from. What's your excuse? Or are you just running from yourself?'

He had this uncanny knack of seeing into her head, and she didn't want to walk away with those eyes on her but had little alternative. She limped to the door and out into the hall. She wasn't going to let a stranger make her feel hurt. She had finished with hurt.

The flight of stairs looked like a mountain but she bit her lips and started. She had stiffened up much more than she had imagined, and her hand on the banister was white with the force of the grip she had to use to pull herself up. The pain-killers weren't working yet either. In the morning she would state her case very determinedly.

She didn't hear him behind her until she was swung into the air, locked in two arms like iron, and panic washed through her again as if she had just arrived here.

She forgot how much he disliked her. She forgot how to cope with this sort of thing. She began to struggle furiously, really too scared to scream, her breath short gasps in her throat.

'Stop it!' He stood perfectly still and glared into her frantic eyes. 'What the hell do you imagine I'm going to do? Coming up these stairs was really hurting you. Do you think I'm altogether heartless? This is a lift only, Miss Shaw. Believe me, I'd do it for anybody and expect no reward at all, and it might calm you to know that there isn't one single reward you could offer to interest me.'

She stopped struggling but her heart was beating madly. His arms seemed to be aggressively possessive, as if she had tried to escape and been caught. The silent house, the isolation, the seemingly ruthless character of the man who held her all combined to bring her close to fainting again, and she gave a queer little moan that was unmistakably terror.

He looked at her frustratedly and then shook his head in exasperation, continuing to climb the stairs with his now subdued burden.

'I wonder if Eric knows his niece is psychotic? You'd better get those nerves under control—unless it's just me?'

It was, she told herself frantically. Even now she was dreading the time when he would put her down and have his hands free.

He carried her until she was actually at her door, which was wide open.

'I can see you're not too good at taking care of yourself,' he muttered, sliding her to her feet as he looked into her room at the pile of bedding. 'Bathroom's down the passage—nothing too luxurious here like *en suite* bathrooms. Go and run your bath and I'll make this bed up.'

'You don't have to. I can do it. You—you called me down for supper before I had time and I ... You really have no need to—to bend over backwards to ...'

'Get your bath ready,' he advised before she could point out that doing this would not take away the fright she felt nor excuse his earlier rudeness. 'From tomorrow Mrs Teal will do it. Let's just say goodnight, Miss Shaw. For now I think I've seen more than enough of you.'

He just started and ignored her, and she collected her things and went along the passage, feeling very uneasy indeed.

It would be all right tomorrow. Mrs Teal would be here, and whatever the woman was like she couldn't be as bad as Jake Garrani. She would stay in the bathroom until he went away and then lock herself in the bedroom. Somehow she had to keep on the right side of him. He was a powerful man and she had to stay here until she had thought out her next move.

The bath helped to soothe both her leg and her frightened feelings. She even managed to smile when she thought of how Mr Skelton would have disapproved of her activities today. After tomorrow, though, she would have an ally in the woman who looked after Uncle Eric; otherwise she would have to slip away from the house and go somewhere else, although right now she had no idea where.

She got dried and listened carefully at the door. There was no sound and she went along to her room quickly, relieved to see he had made her bed and gone. She bent to lock the door, her breath leaving her in a thankful sigh that ended in a gasp.

There was no lock! Panic rushed over her and she had to calm herself quickly. Why should there be a lock? It wasn't a hotel. There had never been locks on the bedrooms at the vicarage until her father had grimly put them there, and there was not one lock on the inside doors of the flat. It was just that she was on edge and this man scared her, she told herself firmly.

She got into bed, staring at the door for a long time, but the house was silent, the soft drip of water falling from the eaves the only sound, and gradually the steady rhythm soothed her until she lay back against the pillows and fell into a deep sleep, the silence of the old house around her and a dark, sardonic face in her mind.

CHAPTER THREE

THE first feeling Emma had on waking was one of astonishment. She had survived the night! With the coming of daylight last night's traumatic events seemed distant and unlikely, and for a few minutes she lay in bed, a smile on her face as she looked around at the room. It was a pleasant room, old-fashioned but somehow comforting. The vicarage had been old-fashioned, the furniture like this, big, old, well polished—her mother had seen to that, though not at St Jude's—her mother had not been there long enough to make a home and she had not even tried. The life had gone out of her.

Emma's eyes clouded as she thought of her father. Events had ruined his life so much more than hers, although nobody had ever known how much. He had faced the whole horror of things while she had been too young to know. All she had felt was a dread, a child's instinctive awareness, and later when she had really known she had locked doors, closed windows, become alert, as her father had told her to. She had learned an attitude to take if ever she should be trapped by some man.

She pushed memory aside and sat up, sliding her legs out of bed and doing what she did first thing every morning now—her exercises. They were hard, sometimes quite painful, but she had not suffered from yesterday's adventures as much as she had anticipated. The leg had eased off during the night. The bed had been warm and comfortable. Nothing had happened to her. Jake Garrani didn't even like her and he was no threat.

She could face black scowls daily with no trouble at all. Smiles were worrying, not scowls.

There was noise downstairs, the smell of freshly cooked breakfast drifted up, and Emma suddenly realised she was hungry, the thought driving her to go along to the bathroom for a wash and then come hastily back to dress.

In jeans and a bright red sweater, she had a defiant feeling, a good feeling to have when she faced Jake Garrani, and in any case she knew they were no longer alone in the house. The daily housekeeper had arrived. She could hear her talking to Jake, and the sound of her cheerful voice gave Emma the nerve to walk straight into the kitchen.

Jake was sitting at the table, eating his breakfast, and at the sight of her he stood politely, reaching across to pull out a chair for her.

'Sleep well?' This morning his eyes were mocking and she knew this polite and solicitous remark was merely for the benefit of the plump women who stood cooking bacon and eggs, her eyes bright and inquisitive on Emma's face.

'Thank you, yes, I did.' Her reply was as brief as his enquiry, and she turned at once to the other occupant of the kitchen. 'You must be Mrs Teal, who keeps house for my uncle.' She was rather proud of that remark; it put Jake Garrani in his place. He was merely staying here; the house belonged to Uncle Eric.

'That I am, love. I know you're Mr Shaw's niece, Emma. He told me you might come ages ago, but even if he hadn't Mr Garrani's been explaining how you arrived last night.'

Emma's eyes shot to Jake's face. Explaining how she had arrived? Had he been telling this woman about her fright and the fainting? There was no way of knowing; then he looked up at her from beneath black brows, and she relaxed. He wouldn't have bothered. He had probably only been driven to explaining because otherwise she would have appeared and startled Mrs Teal.

'Mr Garrani says you hurt your leg last night, dear. I hope it's all right? If you want me to look at it for you...?'

'Oh, no, thank you, Mrs Teal. It's much better today.'

She accepted her breakfast with a ready smile, feeling like a liar, her face slightly flushed, and Jake stood, looked down at her for a second and then walked out without a word.

'I don't think things are going too well at the moment; he's a bit quiet this morning,' Mrs Teal said in a low voice. 'He's an artist.'

'Yes. He's very famous,' Emma informed her.

'Is he?' Mrs Teal absorbed this information with some surprise. 'Of course, we're a bit cut off here from knowing such things. Anyhow, he's a lovely man, famous or not, but, as I say, I don't think things are going too well at the moment. Maybe he doesn't like what he's painting.'

'Er—where does he work?' Emma asked carefully, making a note to find out and thereafter steer clear of the place.

'Same place as your uncle works. There's a studio at the back of the house. Your uncle had it built on years ago. Mind you, the light's not good today, what with this fog. Maybe that's what's making Mr Garrani so quiet.'

Emma didn't think so. She thought it was her. He was irritated because she was here, and if his work was going badly it would only annoy him more. She thought he'd said he hadn't even started yet. Maybe she had mistaken what he had told her last night?

Her fright seemed completely silly today, sitting here with this comfortable woman fussing round her, the smell of breakfast in the cosy kitchen and the lights on against the foggy morning. It all lifted her spirits, until she remembered her plight.

What was she really going to do? She could hardly insist on staying here with Jake Garrani. For one thing, she obviously got on his nerves and, for another, what would Mrs Teal think? It was all right now. She had come unexpectedly, imagining her uncle was there, but that wouldn't do for long. Mrs Teal would expect her to go. The trouble was, she didn't really have any place to go at all.

She couldn't afford to take a flat by herself and she had no one to share with. She knew she couldn't take up her training again yet. It was too strenuous and she could not stand still for very long. Then also there was Gareth. If she went back to London, would he find her? The whole thing was impossible but she had to find a way out.

'Don't you ever think of "living in", Mrs Teal?' she asked, breaking the silence with this stray hope, about to suggest it if Mrs Teal gave her any loophole.

'Bless you, no! I have my own house. I come on my bike, dear. It's not far. I only live at the cottages at the beginning of the moor path.'

She busily got on with her work and Emma sat with her breakfast, her face frustrated. Just how long had she got? Well, there was her car for one thing; that should take a little time.

'Mr Garrani says you've got car trouble,' Mrs Teal said comfortably, breaking into Emma's guilty planning. 'There's nobody here to fix it. Still, I don't expect it matters—Mr Garrani has his car. In fact, I'm glad he has,' she ended with a laugh. 'I forgot one or two things when the grocery man came. Mr Garrani is going to fetch them for me. You could go with him and have a look at the village. It's quite pretty.'

He walked in at that moment, looking as dark and forbidding as usual, but Mrs Teal was not at all put out.

'I've just been telling Miss Shaw she should go with you to the village. She won't have seen anything of it last night in the fog.'

He looked down at Emma irritably.

'It's foggy now. However, if you want to come...'

Not when he'd offered like that she didn't! She glared up at him and one dark brow rose derisively. He obviously thought she'd suggested it herself to wheedle her way round him and stay here.

'Not really. I can go by myself when my car's fixed. I'll phone about it this morning.'

'That's a good idea,' he agreed sardonically, adding, 'there's no garage in the village, though. It's going to cost a lot to have it fixed from what I saw last night. They charge for just coming out too, about thirty pounds with the distance they'll have to come.'

She could tell from the way he was looking at her that he suspected she had little money. Thirty pounds just to turn up! Then there was the repair. It would eat into what little she had. When she looked up, her teeth biting into her lip anxiously, he was watching her intently, and she found her face flushing with embarrassment.

'Well, it sounds reasonable, this place being so isolated,' she lied gallantly. 'I'll call them after breakfast. I expect they're in the book?'

He just nodded and walked out, and she found she couldn't eat another thing.

'I'm going to the village now. Come if you want to.' He was really good at this trick of speaking over his shoulder as if she might or might not be there, and Emma got up and limped after him into the hall.

'There's no need whatever to humour me,' she pointed out angrily, keeping her voice down. 'I don't want to come with you at all, as a matter of fact.'

He almost ignored her, shrugging into a leather jacket and striding to the door.

'Please yourself. Maybe it's best to stay and phone the garage. If they come and fix your car it will be quite possible for you to move out tomorrow.'

So he *was* going to insist that she leave. She stopped quite still in the hall as he slammed the door. He was a hurtful man. If she hadn't got such a grip on herself he could have made her feel tearful. What was she going to do? If it weren't for her bad leg...!

Like an omen the sun suddenly came out, flooding the hall with light, and she made her mind up to get out of the house for a few minutes. Perhaps she could think better in the open air. She went up to her room and collected her warm jacket and a scarf, a red one to boost her spirits again. She was too touchy, what with one thing and another. It was time she let things take their course more, let herself live a little without this constant uptight feeling. Most people were very nice, even men... Gareth had been wonderful.

The thought of another man, a dark, sardonic man, a man who stared into her mind and watched her coldly, made her stiffen up. She had to give more thought to what she would do after tomorrow, but the immediate irritation of Jake Garrani lingered like a storm that threatened. With anyone else she might have put her cards on the table, confessed that she had been relying on Uncle Eric to put her up for a while, just until she was a bit better. She couldn't confess anything to Jake Garrani. There had been antagonism between them from the word go. And now he had actually *said* the word go. She was to leave tomorrow.

As soon as she stepped away from the house Emma realised how cold it was. The fact that the sun was shining didn't detract from the bite in the air and, in any case, away from the confines of the garden, she could see that the sunshine was merely hazy, with no strength to it at all.

The moorland was soft in the haze, soft and secret, bright grassy hillocks and gorse, coarse turf and sharp outcrops of rock the only relief to wild and barren vistas of distance. It was as old as time, rather intimidating but so peaceful that she went on, keeping to the twisting path that led out across the barren landscape, careful as to where she stepped, her eyes rising more and more frequently to look into the distance as the wind stung her cheeks and whipped colour up beneath the pallor of her skin.

It brought back the memory of what it had been like before, when she was healthy and vigorous. Her fears hadn't mattered so much then; she had always known she could run if anything happened. It brought back too a determination to get back to that state of health. She would soon be able to resume her course at the hospital, and then she could move anywhere she liked—there was always room for a qualified physiotherapist.

She had taken the loss of normal movement badly. Not at first. Her accident had been too much of a shock, coming as it had so soon after her father's death. But in retrospect she realised that Gareth had made her feel dependent on him. He had been attentive and persistent, his interest wonderful after her rather lonely childhood and teenage life. She had been gradually trusting him more and more, and when he had told her about his wife she had been shattered. It would be a long time before she even began to recover from that dreadful evening.

She suddenly realised that since she had been here Gareth had hardly entered her mind at all, and she had few doubts about why. Jake Garrani was more than enough to cope with. His aggressive masculinity left no real room for thoughts of anyone else. It was a battle for survival with him, and she was rather pleased with the way she had been able to cope with the fear and the aggression—he hadn't exactly had it all his own way. That kind of battle she could cope with, just as she felt safe alone out here because there was distance, room to escape.

Finally, of course, he would win, because she couldn't stay if he insisted that she go. Did she have the nerve to insist on staying? What would she do if he refused? There was no possibility of going back to the old flat. She had now given up any claim on that, and then there was Roy Duncan. Jake Garrani was better. At least he was openly nasty, with no ulterior motives, and there was no chance of Gareth's finding her here.

So involved with her thoughts that she was miles away in her mind, Emma suddenly realised she had been going for a long time. She twisted round to look back at the house and discovered that the mist had closed in behind her. The house was no longer visible and she stopped, determined not to get into any sort of panic and lose all sense of direction. All she had to do was retrace her steps.

It was then that she discovered too that she had left the path, that she had been walking on soft turf for a long time, and whether she had come in a straight line or not she had no way of telling. She turned about, keeping her head, and made her way back in what she prayed was the right direction. Even then the uppermost thought in her mind was the fact that Jake Garrani would scorn her even more, and she was determined not to give him the opportunity.

It was with a burst of great gladness therefore that she saw Credlestone Hall looming out of the fog, and stepped through the gate on to the stony path. She should have more confidence in herself.

Her confidence faded as Jake suddenly loomed out of the fog too, his dark face furious.

'What the hell do you think you're doing?' he bit out, confronting her like a demon, glaring down from his intimidating height. 'Haven't you any sense at all? You just walk out of the house without a word. How was I expected to find you in this? Dartmoor isn't a small patch of heath. I didn't even know you'd gone out until Mrs Teal told me!'

'I didn't want you to find me,' Emma protested sharply, angry with him immediately. He was standing here, taking her to task when she hardly knew him at all and disliked him with as much intensity as he disliked her. He was going to throw her out tomorrow, so what did it matter to him if she got lost today? 'You have nothing to do with me whatever. I can manage perfectly well alone and, to prove it, here I am,' she finished defiantly.

'Very amusing,' he sneered. 'And what if you hadn't managed by yourself? What if that leg had given out on you? Did you plan to lie in a ditch until the sun shone some time in the future? You've forgotten, I suppose, that there's a prisoner on the run? Am I supposed to ignore the fact that Eric's niece has staggered into my life? What do I say when he comes back—"Sorry, old chap, she was here but I misplaced her"? You'll damned well not move without my consent until tomorrow, and then you'll be on your way!'

'You—you can leave me alone,' Emma managed tremulously, numbed by his ability to say such hurtful things. She was only too aware that she had staggered into his life. She *had* forgotten about the prisoner too. 'I don't need any help at all, and if I did want help it wouldn't be from you.'

'The help you need is from the garage, Miss Shaw,' he reminded her nastily. 'Imagine my surprise when Mrs Teal told me that, as far as she knew, you hadn't even phoned them.'

'I was waiting until I got back,' Emma managed quickly. 'I don't know why she should have given you that information.'

'Because I asked her,' he stated pithily. 'And it then occurred to me that you might have decided to make that leg worse in order to stay right here and drive me mad.'

'I have no desire to stay here. With a bit of luck they'll do the car today and I'll go.' It was clear he would react violently if she suggested anything else. She couldn't throw herself on his non-existent mercy. She might as well face it now and get it over with. She turned and walked up the path, very much aware that he was behind her, watching again. She would never have believed it was possible to hate someone so much on such short acquaintance.

She walked into the hall and picked up the telephone directory, looking through the yellow pages with trembling fingers, and found the nearest garage. She had studied the map long enough to know where it would be.

'I suppose this is the one?' she enquired coldly, reading out the address to Jake. He just stood there, tight-lipped, and nodded, listening while she phoned, making quite sure she was really preparing to go.

They couldn't do it. They were booked up until tomorrow afternoon and they only gave a vague promise about then. No amount of pleading could move them, and when she turned to explain it all to Jake he cut into her words.

'I can hear. They *may* come tomorrow.'

'I'll try somewhere else.'

'Don't bother. I can live through another day, or even two. Leave it as it is.' He walked out, every muscle in him tight with exasperation, and she could see what he meant. In actual fact she had never battled with a man in her whole life before—she had avoided them. It just seemed natural to battle with Jake Garrani. What made him think she could live through another day with *him*, anyway? She wasn't going to beg anything from him and that was for sure. She would rather sleep under a bridge!

Mrs Teal appeared from the kitchen and looked relieved to see her.

'Oh, Miss Shaw, you gave us a fright. There's a lot of fog at this time of the year. It's lucky Mr Garrani came back so quickly. I was scared you might have got yourself lost.'

Emma decided not to tell her she had made it back all by herself. Let him take the credit—he obviously ruled the place and everyone in it. By tomorrow night, with any luck, he would be a bad memory. As to giving him a fright as well as Mrs Teal, he wasn't worrying about her at all. If he was at all concerned it was because he was just worried about what to do if she became Emma Shaw—deceased!

It was a very subdued lunchtime, and then Jake simply stalked off and left her with Mrs Teal, who was in any case too busy to chatter. Emma wandered around, inspecting her uncle's house, ending up in the sitting-room with a small pile of books she had found and curling up in front of a glowing fire. The fog was now back as if it had never gone away at all, and Mrs Teal finally stuck her head in the door and informed her with a smile that there was a quiche for tonight, the salad was already made and there was a nice fruit salad to follow and a good soup for starters.

It all sounded very pleasant and Emma stretched out on the settee, her leg comfortable, the fire cosy, and she was not even slightly anxious when later she heard the front door close firmly and saw Mrs Teal wheeling her cycle down the stony path. It brought a shudder. She wouldn't have liked to be cycling across the moor this evening. For all she knew, that prisoner was still on the loose. She would have to see that she left early when her car was done. For now, though, she was warm and comfortable, and when she found her eyelids closing drowsily she astonished herself by just letting it happen.

The sound of the curtains being drawn brought her partly back to wakefulness, and she opened her eyes to see Jake's tall frame by the window as he closed the curtains against the foggy evening.

'Sorry I disturbed your beauty sleep,' he murmured as she sat up, feeling slightly disorientated. 'Not a good idea anyway. You'll never sleep tonight.' She came right out of her dreams then and swung her legs downwards, her face slightly flushed from sleep. He didn't look quite so cross, and that in itself was worrying.

'Want a drink?' He came and stood looking down at her, his eyes dark and thoughtful.

'No, well—if you mean a drink then no, but I would like some tea. I'll make it.' She began to stand but he put his hand on her shoulder, keeping her there.

'I'll do it. We'll both have tea.'

He sounded annoyed again and she hastily corrected any impression she might have given. 'I wasn't meaning—I mean, I don't mind if you want to have a drink. It's just that I'm not used to... I can make my own tea.' Her voice trailed away as he stared down at her.

'I wasn't thinking of drinking myself into a stupor. I'm quite happy to have tea. I'm also going to make it. I'm not really the dreamy-artist type who can't find his shirt.'

He walked off and she sank back on the settee. No, he wasn't dreamy. He was unfathomable and irritating, unnerving and cold, and he had stoked up the fire. He must have been quiet doing that, and it made her feel very anxious to think he had actually been here, close by, when she was asleep. Her fears threatened to surface again but she considered things carefully. He hadn't done a thing and she was still safe.

How strange he was. Some people were not capable of being warm at all. Maybe he couldn't help it? She cheered up and sat a little straighter, her face resolutely pleasant when he came back into the room. If she could teach him some manners her living would not have been in vain. The thought brought a half-smile to her face.

'Completely back among the living, I see,' he murmured, almost wiping the pleasure from her face until he added, 'Feel better?'

'Yes, thank you.' She looked into her tea as he handed her a cup, and then decided to be perfectly truthful. 'Actually I was very nearly lost. I got off the path and the fog came back quickly without my knowing. I was relieved to see you.'

There! It was a big effort for her but she *had* tried. Maybe if she could get on a bit better with him he would let her stay, she thought guiltily.

'Were you?' He sat down and looked across at her derisively. 'You've decided, then, have you, that I'm not after all intent on either murdering you or raping you?'

She went perfectly still, her face instantly white, the cup shaking in her hand, but she kept her nerve. Once again she was reminded that they were alone, and her earlier fears tried hard to surge back.

'I—I'm not at all worried,' she began.

'You are. Now that Mrs Teal's left you're back to terror.' He suddenly stood, making her jump warily, but all he was doing was standing against the mantelpiece, and her eyes moved over his tall, lean figure, her breathing not quite steady. There was something about him that... 'You're all right with me, Emma Shaw. I don't desire you and I'm not at all murderous. I also keep your uncle in mind. I may want to borrow this house again.'

He was smiling slightly and she took a few deep breaths while he watched her, his gaze going to her tightly clenched hands. She felt tight inside, unbearably anxious. Jake Garrani was almost vibrating with masculinity. It was the thing she had noticed right from the first. It alarmed her most of the time, and right now it almost choked her.

'I'm well aware that I'm all right with you,' she assured him as calmly as possible. 'If I weren't I would have left when Mrs Teal went. In any case, I assume that you're respectable. My uncle wouldn't know you if you weren't.'

His dark brows rose a little at that rather naïve remark, but he said nothing and she moved with what she imagined looked like impatience—she hoped it did, anyway.

'There's no need to stand watching me, Mr Garrani. I'm not about to either faint or scream.'

She knew she was being unnecessarily sharp, quite nasty really, but she couldn't help it. She was programmed to protect herself, and he went back to his seat, his brows drawn together in the old scowl she had quite got used to.

'OK! It's none of my business what you do. All I wanted to do was state my intentions, which don't actually exist, as I've pointed out.'

'I'm sorry, I——'

'Forget it!' he ordered coldly. 'After tomorrow we'll never see each other again. I don't have time to psychoanalyse you.'

Now she had no idea what to say. All her good resolutions had gone.

'I'll get the supper.' She glanced at her watch, seeing that it was almost seven. It was a good excuse to get out of the room, and he shrugged.

'Why not? You may as well make yourself useful while you're here.' The hardness was back with a vengeance, and she made a great effort and walked from the room, well aware that his eyes followed her, her nervousness making her far too conscious of a limp that was, after all, only temporary.

In the quiet of the kitchen she thought about it. How temporary? Mr Skelton had made no definite promises, and how could he? It had been a very bad accident and she knew herself he had already worked miracles; with a lesser man, she would have been completely crippled for life.

She set the table, her face rather grim as she thought things over, and when she looked up Jake was leaning in the doorway, watching her, his tall dark frame darker still in black trousers and shirt.

'I changed for dinner,' he pointed out wryly when she just looked at him, her own heartbeats surprising her when she noticed the very virile and handsome picture he made, leaning there. It wasn't at all like the way Roy Duncan had leaned in the doorway when he came to the flat to see Sue. This was no studied pose. Jake was just being a man. The thought shocked her and she blushed suddenly, looking away.

'Very good,' she assured him primly. 'I haven't changed because, for one thing, all my clothes are creased and, for another, I couldn't be bothered. You'll have to eat with me as I am, or I could go and eat in my room if I'm too off-putting.'

'Ah! Spirit!' he commented sardonically, coming across and sitting down, his eyes keenly on her blushes. 'It suits you better than the Marley's Ghost act.'

'I was—*am* spirited!' Emma said emphatically, bringing the salad to the table and setting it down.

'A Freudian slip,' he noted. '"Was" has become "am". I take the credit. I've goaded you into it.'

For the first time a slow smile moved across his mouth, growing until his dark face was alight with laughter, a devastatingly handsome face when he wasn't glowering. He sat looking up at her, the smile playing around his lips, and now she was the one who glowered. It was as bad when he laughed at her as when he snarled.

'You've certainly goaded. I know I was unexpected, but manners are cheap, after all, Mr Garrani. But don't bother to be too complacent. I'm leaving tomorrow.'

'I haven't forgotten, Miss Shaw,' he said in a deceptively soft voice. 'Apparently we're both counting the hours.'

She sat down, her annoyance suddenly gone as she thought of the morning. What on earth was she going to do? She hadn't come up with a single place to go. Where was there, after all? He began to eat silently, his eyes for once giving her a bit of peace, and she knew she had to make an effort now. Later she just wouldn't have the courage.

'I know this is going to annoy you,' she said quietly, going on with a rush when she felt his startled eyes come to her bent head, 'but I want to stay here. After all, if my uncle had been here there would have been no problem. It isn't as if you're renting the house. You're just a guest, as am I. Uncle Eric certainly wouldn't have thrown me out, and I can't really see how I would get in your way. I—I mean if I helped Mrs Teal, served the meal each night and generally stayed in the background...'

She ran out of steam, and he was so quiet that she dared not look up. She had stated her case, but she couldn't stay if he insisted otherwise. For one thing, he was a lot bigger than she was.

'Are you telling me you've got no place to go?' the dark voice probed.

'Well—not right away. I can't go back to my flat because there's someone there and...'

'You can stay,' he said quietly as her voice trailed into silence. 'I don't want you helping Mrs Teal, though. You can help me.'

It was Emma's turn to look up, startled, but he was getting on with his meal.

'Help you? How could I possibly...?'

'Pose for me,' he suggested, his dark eyes glancing up and capturing her gaze.

CHAPTER FOUR

THE thought of that painting on television flashed into Emma's mind, and her face flushed brightly.

'I—I couldn't *possibly* . . .!'

Jake grimaced, his mouth twisting wryly.

'You don't know much, do you, Little Miss Shaw? I can tell you categorically that I've never painted a duchess nude—not once—and with *you*, I wouldn't even think about it. It was not an immoral question. You can keep your clothes on.'

The look he gave her assured her that to him she would be even more uninteresting without clothes than she was fully dressed. Colour flared under her skin even more, and he made an impatient gesture with his hand, frustration with her written clearly on his face.

'You're too good to miss.'

'What do you mean, too good to miss?'

'You've been ill, I can see that; you're almost fragile. You've suffered, too, recently, and that's not just the artistic eye. All added together with your long black hair, your dark blue eyes, that look on the edge of tears a lot of the time, and you're too good to miss. It's as simple as that.'

'You're—you're cruel!' She stared at him in angry horror and he looked right back.

'Probably.' He shrugged dismissively. 'I normally paint people who have plenty of money to spend on my portraits. People who are wealthy and spoiled, self-indulgent and self-satisfied. I told you I came here to escape too much commercial work. That's the commercial work. It's not often I get the chance to do exactly as I like. You're haunting. I want to paint you. Agree and you can stay as long as you like with no opposition. I'll ignore your peculiarities.'

'You mean you want to paint an oddity?' Emma said bitterly, her flushed face now quite pale.

He held her gaze. She had no idea how stricken she looked. His eyes roamed over her face, calculating and unemotional, sizing her up for the canvas. 'You're beautiful,' he said coldly and flatly.

He went back to his meal as if that remark was of no importance, and she imagined it was not important to him. He was looking at it all from a workmanlike point of view. Nobody had ever called her beautiful before, though, even Gareth. It gave her a small glow inside that was different from anything she had ever felt. Jake Garrani painted plenty of beautiful women, and he had been looking at her with an artist's eyes.

'Well?' His eyes demanded, and she came to her senses.

'No.' She looked away, her lips tightening from the parted, soft and startled look they had taken on. In the first place, she didn't altogether trust him and, in the second place, she didn't want to be sitting watching him for hours on end—she wanted to keep out of his way. In the third place, she couldn't sit still for so long—her leg wouldn't allow it.

'Why? Have you something more pressing to do, or have you suddenly realised you have a Mayfair flat after all?'

He sounded cold again, scathing, and she stood, turning for the door, wanting to walk off and forget about this.

'I don't need to stay,' she lied coolly. 'In any case, I don't like sitting still for long periods of time. I get quite bored.'

She moved, but he was behind her in a flash, standing and moving before she realised it, his hands hard and firm on her slender shoulders.

'I badly want to paint you,' he grated. 'Stop pretending you've got somewhere to go. It's pretty damned obvious you haven't.' He took a deep breath that sounded as if he was making a great effort to control his temper. 'I'll make it easy for you. I realise perfectly well you can't sit still for a long time. I know you're lame.'

Emma spun round to deny it, shocked to find his face was so close to hers, and he went on before she could get out any other sort of lie.

'I watched you coming up the path when we first arrived. You were limping long before you stumbled on the step.'

'I—I wasn't and——'

'You were. You obviously didn't want me to know, so I've never mentioned it because it's none of my business. You don't have to pretend with me. It's not important; I mean, it doesn't matter—your being lame.'

His hands were moulding her shoulders almost absentmindedly, making her warm, and it scared her.

'It—it's only temporary. I'm not always going to be lame,' she said defensively. 'I had an accident. A car knocked me down, but Mr Skelton says that——'

'Never mind Mr Skelton,' he cut in. 'Even if it's permanent, it doesn't make you any less beautiful to paint. I want to paint you. I'll make it really easy for you, just short sessions, and we'll stop whenever you say.'

'I don't know,' Emma murmured worriedly. 'It seems wrong to just—just come here right out of the blue and meet you and then agree to. . .'

He threw his head back with a great gesture of impatience, half turning away but then spinning round to pin her with dark, irritated eyes.

'Look!' he snapped. 'People meet and fall in love at first glance, marry within days. I'm only asking you to pose for a picture. Do we have to exchange credentials and introductions for that? An artist grasps what he needs, and right now I need you. Before you came I was going around like a bear with a sore head, no idea what to paint.' He stuck his hand out imperiously and grasped hers, shaking it with irritated vigour. 'I'm Jake Garrani, Miss Shaw. How are you?' He glared at her. 'That's all the introduction you're going to get. Now, do we have a bargain or not?'

'I—I don't know.' She looked up at him, almost open-mouthed. Who knew what this man would do next? As far as she could tell, he was permanently like a bear with a sore head. 'You'll probably be disappointed anyway.'

'Disappointed with my own efforts? I'm Garrani!' he pointed out arrogantly.

'I didn't mean that. What I meant was that model—the one who was in the painting on television—she was so beautiful and...'

It didn't have a good effect on him at all. Anger sliced across his dark face.

'Leave her out of this! I wanted to get rid of that portrait. I would have given it away!' He obviously struggled to regain his temper, not wanting to lose an interesting oddity to paint. 'Look, sit down again and eat your meal.'

He led her back to the table and helped her into her seat, sitting opposite and watching her for a second before going on.

'The portrait I do of you will be my best ever. I can *feel* it!' His strong sensitive fingers came across the table and grasped hers almost cruelly. 'I've told you you're beautiful. I mean it. Believe me, I rarely say that. Praise from Garrani tends to make heads swell. Pose for me and I'll buy you this damned house!'

His intensity was too overwhelming. It certainly over-whelmed Emma and had her staring at him in awe.

'Well? Will you?' he rasped impatiently.

'I'll try.'

'You won't *try*, Miss Shaw! If you sit for me you'll stay the distance. I don't give up a portrait halfway through. Back out after I've started and I'll probably strangle you. Make your mind up right now!'

Did he imagine she could still speak after this on-slaught? All Emma could do was nod, and when he stared at her furiously with those dark eyes she found her voice.

'I'll do it if I can stay.'

'Stay? You'll never get away once I've started, so forget any accommodation problems. Now finish your meal and go to bed—I want to get things set up for morning.'

He looked quite fanatical, and Emma felt an odd shiver of alarm.

'Don't let me scare you.' His face closed instantly and he made a great effort to smile quite pleasantly. 'Artists are weird people sometimes. I'm now fired with enthusiasm.'

He looked away and got on with his meal, silent until she relaxed and ate hers too, but something was bub-bling inside him, she could feel it, and it gave her a sharp thrill to realise that she had inspired this clever and tal-ented man—a world-famous painter.

He turned her to the door as soon as she had finished and, although she felt embarrassed that he watched her walking, it wasn't nearly as bad as she had thought. It was a relief that he knew. She wouldn't have to pretend any more. She had her other problem solved too. She could stay here.

'About your fee,' he suddenly said as she got to the stairs.

'No!' Emma swung round and faced him. If she had a fee she would feel obliged to stay until it was all finished, and she might not be able to stand him that long.

'What do you mean, no? Models expect a fee; it's the first thing they say.'

'Well, I'm not a model. I'm doing this so that I can stay and—and to help you out, as you're so... so...'

'Inspired?' he enquired wryly. 'Listen, Miss Shaw, this is your uncle's house. You can stay as long as you like and we both know it.'

'But you said that...'

'That I wanted to get rid of you? I did, before I decided to paint you. The last thing I want is a woman hanging around.'

'I'll still be a woman when you're painting me.' It was startling the way he said exactly what he wanted to say with no thought of subterfuge.

'No, you won't. You'll be a model, an inanimate object. You'll also get bullied. So what about your fee?'

'No fee,' Emma said firmly. 'I'm doing this as a favour. Just remember that when you're trying to bully me because I certainly won't stand for it.'

Emma raised her chin and looked at him steadily, and she was suddenly at the receiving end of a very unexpected grin.

'We'll see.' He turned away and she got another of those 'over the shoulder' remarks. 'I want you down here bright and early in the morning.'

He was bullying already. He must be awful to work for in normal circumstances. Still, he wasn't exactly an enemy any more, and she had a roof over her head. Things seemed a little more safe than they had been last night, although if anyone was odd it was Jake Garrani.

It was sunny again as she opened her eyes next morning and she stretched, smiling a secret smile as the words

Jake had said rang in her ears. 'You're beautiful...it doesn't matter—your being lame.' This morning it *didn't* matter, and she seemed to have slept better than she had done for a whole year, even longer than that.

She swung her legs out of bed and stood, testing her leg, and then sat again to do her exercises. Her knee wasn't nearly so painful today. It was a good omen. Maybe it would soon be better.

There was a knock on the door and Jake's voice surprised her.

'Emma? Hurry up. The light's good and I want to get started.'

It was promising that he was calling her Emma in a better voice. Should she call him Jake? That would take some doing. She only had to hear his voice to get jumpy, but she had her own set routine and she wasn't going to let him hustle her.

'I'll be down soon,' she called firmly.

'What's wrong with immediately?' he demanded irritably, and it irritated her too.

'I have exercises to do and nothing stops me.' Really! He was quite impossible.

'*Exercises*?' He opened the door and came to stand just inside before she could even move. 'What's this female nonsense? Am I supposed to wait around while you tone up and move to music?'

He hadn't even given her time to get into her robe, and she had never had a man appearing in her room before. The white satin of her nightie seemed to be no covering at all.

'It's not toning up and I don't move to music!' she snapped, hastily reaching for her robe. 'I have exercises to do for my leg, and if I don't do them then I'll never get better. If you don't want to wait you can——!'

'All right, all right!' He looked a bit rueful, his long fingers rubbing the back of his neck, a twisted smile trying to appear on his dark face. 'I didn't know you did exercises. There's no need to go for me like a tigress.'

'Well, you just assume the worst all the time, and you come bursting in here and...!'

His dark eyes were wide open, his eyebrows raised as he watched her flushed face.

'Now that would *really* make a portrait,' he said softly. 'Trouble is, I'd have to keep you in a permanent state of annoyance and I'm not at all sure I could manage it.'

He walked out and closed the door, and she caught sight of herself in the mirror of the dressing-table. Her face was flushed and wild, her eyes wide and deep blue. The white of the nightie accentuated the colouring, and her hair was black and shining, dishevelled. She looked as if she had just been struggling in somebody's arms.

A deep, painful flush coloured her even more when she saw exactly what Jake had seen. She would never be able to pose for him. He had a way of looking into her head that was almost sensual. He scared her in an entirely different way from any other man.

It took a good deal of firm resolve to go down to breakfast; in fact, she lingered until she heard Mrs Teal's voice. Jake was already there, sitting at the table, looking very impatient, but he smiled as she came into the room, very wary about upsetting her, apparently. The thought that for once she had the upper hand with this powerful and unpredictable man brought a secret smile to her face, and he looked at her steadily, his own lips quirking, giving her the impression that he knew exactly what she was thinking. He had rather long lips, she noticed. When he smiled like that they turned down slightly at the corners. She looked away quickly. She had never studied a man before and it seemed to be just asking for trouble.

'Have you got a dark dress?' he enquired unexpectedly. 'Something flowing, preferably grey?'

'I've got a sort of grey-blue dress.' Emma looked across at him seriously and he nodded with satisfaction.

'That will do. The red scarf you wore yesterday too. We'll probably tie that around your waist. The colour's good on you and it will add that unexpected bright spot.'

Even now, Emma could hardly believe it was actually going to happen, but she managed to look quite serious and professional. Mrs Teal served their breakfast, keeping quiet but obviously bursting with enquiry.

'She's going to pose for me, Mrs Teal.' Jake gave the news emphatically and then got on with his meal.

'My! That's nice. Have you got an idea, then?' Clearly she was happy that he would be working away and no longer impatient with himself.

'Several!' He didn't look up, but Emma remembered his parting shot as he had left her room. Colour rose softly under her skin and she was glad neither of them seemed to notice.

'Well, it will keep you off that moor, Miss Shaw.' The housekeeper apparently was all for this latest idea. 'If you're starting straight after breakfast I'd better tell you that lunch will be early today. Twelve-thirty sharp, so make allowances for that. I have a few extra things to do today and I know what artists are like once they get started. I have trouble enough with your uncle,' she added for Emma's benefit, 'never knows when to stop once he's got going.'

Emma looked a little worried, and Jake said firmly, 'This is a new and inexperienced model, Mrs Teal. I'll have to break her in slowly. We'll be finished long before twelve-thirty.'

Emma hoped so, but there was that fanatical look in his eyes again and she knew she might have to be very firm with him. Even that lifted her spirits. Before this she would have shrunk from the idea of being firm with Jake or any man. He didn't scare her quite so much now, though, only when he looked at her too closely. In fact, she was beginning to think she had been scaring herself, her memories too close to the surface after her rather alarming drive across the moor.

It was interesting to go to the studio at the back of the house and see where her uncle had worked for so many years. Since childhood she had known about him. He had never come but her father had always received a copy of any new book he had illustrated and with each book had come a letter. She had sat for hours, entranced by the animals he had drawn and painted, entranced too by the letters her father would read out, stories of Uncle Eric's encounters with wildlife. Many of the illustrations she had come to know so well were there on the studio walls, framed reminders of the endless patience that had made him so famous.

Jake went immediately to his easel and she wandered around, gazing at the illustrations that adorned the walls.

'Good, isn't he?' Jake murmured, busily setting his things out. 'Have you seen them before?'

'Yes. We had most of his books at home. I've got them now but they're crated. I didn't have room for them after...'

'Where did you live—in London, I mean, after your father died?'

It was easier to talk to him when he got on with his work and just muttered at her as he was doing now, and she answered without thinking much about it, never bothering to look around.

'I shared a flat with a nurse—well, she was training, just as I was. It was fairly successful at first, although we didn't have much in common.'

'So what put the cat among the pigeons?' It was dropped in so quietly that she never gave her answer a thought.

'To be frank, a creep called Roy Duncan. He's Sue's boyfriend and he's moved in with her.'

'You disapproved?'

'Yes. It was bad enough when he just called for her—he gave me the shudders. He used to make remarks to me and...'

Emma suddenly realised just what she was saying, blurting her thoughts out to a stranger, and her face flushed as she turned and found that he was not preparing anything at all. He was watching her intently, a sketch pad in his hand, his fingers flying over the page.

'You've started!' It gave her a fright. She hadn't got herself mentally prepared yet and, in any case, he always seemed to be looking at her. 'I was waiting for you to tell me to pose.'

'No need to get annoyed or anxious,' he murmured, his fingers still busily sketching. 'I wanted a few preliminary sketches, and with you wandering around I've been able to get a few from different angles. I'll use them when I need them; it gives extra depth when I know what the back of your head looks like.'

'I see.' She looked doubtful and he suddenly smiled.

'Do you?' He put the pad down and signalled to her. 'Come here. We'll get you set and make a start. I've already prepared your throne.'

He had brought a settee into the room and draped it with material, some sort of dark blue cloth. She held her nerves in check by wondering where he had got it from and trying to figure out which room was now one settee short.

'Is—isn't it going to be too dark? I mean, this grey-blue dress, this dark blue background...'

'It's not the real background,' he muttered a trifle impatiently, urging her towards the settee, clearly not interested in her opinions. 'The background is in my head. *You* are in my head. I've used this because it's the only material not utterly off-putting that had any size to it. Eric doesn't keep things like that around. Birds and beasts don't pose on settees.'

She sat rather primly and he began to move her, his actions so impersonal that by the time he had her arranged she was quite amused to think that he had pushed and pulled her, lifted and twitched her about with so little feeling that she was quite untroubled. She certainly was an inanimate object to him, and that was good because it didn't worry her.

He worried her then.

'Stretch your right leg more,' he snapped as he stood back and regarded her as if she were a vase.

She did it wrongly, of course, and he strode over impatiently, taking her ankle in his hand and moving her to the position he wanted. It didn't bother her too much until his hand came to her skirt, and then she stiffened all over.

'Stay calm,' he muttered, his eyes flashing to her startled face. 'Think of me as Skelton.'

'He's a lot older!' she said unwisely.

'Hmm! How does that make him safe?' he murmured absently as he stood back and observed her pose with a critical frown. 'Let me tell you, Miss Shaw, that older men are often extremely lecherous.'

'That's a terrible thing to say!' Emma gasped, her eyes shocked.

'It settled your nerves, though, didn't it?' he mused with a brief and wintry smile. 'I'll have to keep thinking up shocking things to tell you. I'm sure to get a very reproachful reaction, which beats the trembling fear any day.'

He stood and looked down at her fiercely.

'Now. All by yourself and with no help at all, unfasten the first two buttons of that dress.'

She blushed and looked up at him but she did it anyway, her eyes a mixture of embarrassment and annoyance. It appeared to bring on an attack of sardonic amusement. At any rate, the lean dark face struggled with the need to burst into laughter.

He arranged her scarf and looked closely at her.

'Right! Head back. Perfect! Let's see if you can hold that pose.'

He was all businesslike, and her heart returned to a normal beat as he strode off behind the easel.

'Comfortable?' he murmured and, though she said that she was, she knew he wasn't listening; he appeared to have forgotten about her. He was already working and he was another character entirely.

Emma forgot too. Within minutes she was in what was a new world for her, a world where a dark intent man glanced up at her every few seconds and looked at her as if she weren't there at all. She was lured into watching him, her eyes wide as she noticed so many things about him that she hadn't noticed before.

He was pretty much a perfect specimen of manhood. There was an elegance about him that came from the way he stood, the way he moved, but there was nothing soft about him. He didn't look at all like her preconceived notions of the great artist. His movements were quick, strong and graceful. The dark eyes were deep set, his black brows a bit alarming, and he pulled faces too, odd little movements of his mouth when he was concentrating, his white teeth biting down into his lip from time to time.

He seemed to be working at an alarming rate. They had said on television that he worked fast and she could see what they meant. As he turned to get more paint she noticed how his hair brushed his collar. Did he always keep it like that? It suited him. He glanced up sharply again, his eyes for once meeting hers, his face darkening as she suddenly flushed. He had this uncanny knack of looking at her as if he could read her mind, and she had been sitting here, unashamedly admiring him. That thought made her blush more because it gave her pause for thought.

She had been watching Jake as a man only, speculating about him. She looked down and his voice cracked out at once, coolly impersonal.

'Look up! Don't move!'

It jolted her back to her senses, and after a time she resolutely looked through him instead of at him. It made her aware, though, of her leg, and she wanted to complain a little, but she kept still and said nothing.

It was Jake who decided when she had had enough. He suddenly stopped and put his brush down.

'Relax,' he murmured, his eyes on his own work. 'You can move now. We'll take a coffee break.'

He strode to the door, and to her astonishment he just roared at the top of his voice, 'Mrs Teal! Coffee!'

Emma was stunned, staring at him with her mouth open.

'We can go along there. She'll not like to be bawled at.'

'I'm an artist. I do as I like. It's what people expect.' He came and surprised her by grinning down at her, and Mrs Teal called back so cheerfully that Emma was shocked all over again.

'What did I tell you? People expect it of me. She'd be disappointed if I behaved normally. Ease off. Swing your feet down,' he ordered. 'I know exactly how to get you back to the right pose.'

'Can I see what you've done?' she asked eagerly but he shook his head, the smile dying immediately, as if she had been very impertinent.

'Nobody, but nobody looks at my work until it's finished.'

'Not even your models?' She wondered how that other woman had been able to sit without clothes and stare at Jake. She wondered what it felt like inside. She had never thought anything like that before in her whole life and she looked flustered. He evidently followed her chain of thought again, her looks giving him the necessary clue.

'Those without a title are usually too busy getting dressed, unless they're paying for it. Even then, some of them wouldn't mind.' He was back to derision and it annoyed her at once because he was deliberately trying to embarrass her and she refused to let him.

'You paint everyone nude unless they're a duchess?' she asked tartly. 'It must be very limiting, even for a talented and famous artist.'

She expected an outburst at that, but he looked down at her and laughed softly.

'Well, *touché*, Miss Shaw!' he murmured. 'Before too long you won't have one single inhibition left.'

She was glad to see Mrs Teal with the coffee, returning the beaming smile she got from the housekeeper and avoiding Jake's eyes. It didn't take long for him to annoy her at any time. She wondered how she was ever able to speak to him. He was impossible.

'Walk around as you drink your coffee,' Jake ordered, taking the cup and putting it safely down. 'Come on.'

He simply hauled her to her feet, and she lost balance with the quick movement, falling against him. He caught her, his arm coming round her waist, and for a second she felt the heat and power of his body. The smell of aftershave came faintly to her nostrils, mixing with a scent that was pure male, and a strange feeling raced over her skin, keeping her still. She found herself looking into eyes that were closer than they had ever been, eyes that were deeply brown but flecked with gold, thick dark lashes spiking around them.

'All right?'

There was a rough edge to the sound of his voice that she didn't understand, and she looked hastily away, standing upright, her body tensed.

'Thank you.' It took all her dignity to put things back to normal and he drew back, watching her as she moved jerkily, a tightness about her that showed nothing but alarm. She picked up her coffee and began to walk about.

'Is it going to be too much for you, do you think?' Jake asked quietly, and it didn't please her, not after the odd feelings that were even now roaming around inside her. While she had been sitting there, looking at him, she had felt normal. Now she felt like a cripple and a freak. The thought sharpened her voice.

'It is not going to be too much for me. I'm not in any way an invalid!'

'As you wish,' he retorted tightly. 'I'm taking my break in my room. You can keep walking and we'll get back to it in twenty minutes exactly.'

She nodded and he took her arm, swinging her round none too gently.

'You can do your walking out in the hall or else-where,' he rasped.

'You don't trust me not to look at the painting?' she asked angrily.

'Why should I? There's not a lot of trust flying around.'

'Just because you're painting me it doesn't make you any different,' she snapped, dismayed but not surprised by his return to annoyance, although she had brought it on herself.

'You imagined it would?' he asked scathingly. 'My character was formed before you were even born. I'm quite at home with it.'

He walked out and clearly expected her to follow. She wouldn't have stayed there now for anything in the world anyway.

She was right there, though, waiting by the door when he came lightly down the stairs twenty minutes later.

'All breathless and eager?' he asked sardonically and she absolutely refused to rise to the bait.

'I promised to pose. Here I am, on time.'

'A perfect model,' he murmured drily, leading her in.

She set herself up too, looking at him defiantly and unbuttoning the regulation two buttons, even twitching her skirt higher, as he had done. He brought out any latent ability she had to fight. Her feelings for him now were bordering on a sort of low-simmering hatred.

'That's almost right.' He walked over and slightly rearranged her pose. 'And now, if you don't mind, as you're in a self-controlled mood...'

His fingers flicked open another button and slid the dress slightly off her shoulder, and she held her breath, determined not to panic. He altered the drape of the scarf, his eyes firmly on his arrangements, and it was only as he finished that those dark eyes flashed across her neck and shoulders, lingering where the swell of her breast showed with a tantalising curve.

His eyes met hers and she gazed back fiercely, ignoring the way her colour came and went. She was well aware that he was trying to frighten her, and she was perfectly safe—Mrs Teal was not too far away and, in any case, she knew he was doing it for no other reason than sheer meanness.

'Good girl.'

Suddenly his dark head bent, and he kissed her startled lips very lightly, his cool, strong hand cupping her cheek for a second. Then he was right across the room, behind his easel, and she began to breathe properly again, more bewildered than dismayed, her lips and cheek tingling. He wasn't going to like the effect at all because she knew she must look different.

He didn't seem to mind, though, because after a while his lips curved in a smile, slow and dark, amusement in his voice as he spoke.

'How old are you, Emma?' he asked, his eyes intent on his work.

'Twenty-two.'

'And never been kissed,' he murmured, his eyes flicking to her face without really seeing her as a person, his hand busy and skilled.

'You assume a lot, Mr Garrani,' she managed coolly, thankful to be sitting down and not standing on trembling legs.

'Possibly.' His eyes narrowed as he looked at her critically and then resumed his task. 'Not about you, though, Emma Shaw.' He smiled to himself. 'But you survived it fairly well. I'm proud of you.'

It made her feel about fourteen, and she snapped out at him. 'Which goes to prove that I'm not quite as naïve as you imagine. The kiss didn't trouble me at all.'

'It wasn't a kiss, though. It was merely a salute to your courage. If I really kissed you the result would be somewhat different.'

'I've been kissed before, thank you!'

The dark eyes suddenly looked up, holding hers, his lips twisting sardonically as she hastily looked away.

'Not very seriously, I would say, or perhaps not very skilfully.'

'You know nothing about me, Mr Garrani. I've told you very little. If you imagine there has been no man in my life at my age...'

'Oh, I wouldn't think that. We live in easygoing times. But you're not easygoing, are you?' He just kept on working through this embarrassing exchange, and the cool way he stood there, taking her apart, really angered her.

'I have no wish to be.' She wanted to get up and walk out, but she dreaded his sarcasm if she did and, after all, this was a bargain. If she walked off he would toss her out or make life even more uncomfortable.

'Don't let someone like that smarmy boy who knows your friend put you off, Emma,' he muttered vaguely, his mind now quite obviously back to the portrait. 'To be in a man's arms is sheer joy.'

'For the man.' She wanted him to stop talking at all costs. It was making her feel strange.

He glanced up, a slight frown back on his face at the tight sound of her voice. 'All the world loves a lover,' he murmured. 'A good percentage of the world is made up of women. The joy comes when the right man and the right woman meet.'

The only way to stop this was to keep silent, and Emma closed her lips tightly, staring ahead as if he weren't there. Not that he bothered about that. He had already lost interest in the conversation.

CHAPTER FIVE

WORKING with Jake became easier. During the following week he slowed down the pace, a different movement in his hands as he worked silently. He hardly spoke to Emma at all, and much of her time was spent in simply watching him. As far as he was concerned, she was quite obviously a vase of flowers or an ornate teapot, and she relaxed. Thoughts that amused her sometimes flashed into her mind, and when they did he rapped out at her, telling her not to smile, although she was always astonished that he noticed.

He made sure she was comfortable, keeping the room warm and keeping the sessions down to reasonable lengths. Mrs Teal seemed to thrive on the new atmosphere. She had fathomed out for herself that Emma was lame, and her attitude became even more motherly. Emma relaxed in the peculiar familiarity of being close to Jake, but it seemed to wash right over his head.

He was rarely caustic now, but she knew it was because he didn't want to upset her. If she refused to continue he would have a half-finished canvas on his hands. Even so, the derision was only just beneath the surface, although he kept a tight rein on the acid tongue.

It was almost ten days after they had begun that he suddenly threw down his brush halfway through the morning and swore viciously under his breath.

'Has it gone wrong?' She instantly felt anxious for him, not wanting him to be disappointed, and he glared at her for a second as if her soft tones irritated him.

'No. I've run out of colour. Utter stupidity! It's something I don't do.' He wiped his brush and his fingers, shrugging resignedly. 'Still, I suppose I can excuse myself to some extent. I don't normally work at the back of nowhere in a house surrounded by fog.'

'It's sunny today,' Emma ventured soothingly, remembering belatedly that she was supposed to be exercising in the fresh air and not just sitting still, as she had done for over a week with ever-increasing willingness. And what was she doing, soothing Jake? It never made any difference to him what she did.

'Good job!' he snapped, glancing at the window. 'I'll have to go to Tavistock for more paint. I might even have to go to Plymouth.' He stretched and ran his hand through his hair. 'That lets work out for today.' He strode to the door, pausing to make one of his normal over-the-shoulder remarks. 'Tell Mrs Teal I'll get lunch out today. I'd better start now.'

He had so obviously dismissed her from his mind that Emma felt a wave of dismay. It was ridiculous, but she was beginning to look forward to seeing him. The thought of a whole day without his irritating presence around made her feel crushed. She would be lonely.

She hurried after him into the hall.

'Jake! Can I come with you?'

He was already on his way upstairs and he paused, looking down at her in surprise, his dark eyes on her hopeful face.

'Better not.' His encompassing glance seemed to take in the way she stood stiffly, her weight on her good leg, and the hope drained out of her expression as she turned away. He was out of sight up the stairs before she had made it to the privacy of the sitting-room, and suddenly it didn't look inviting any more. There was no fire yet, for one thing, and Mrs Teal hadn't got around to this room. Last night's occupancy was still hanging in the air, the remains of the fire, Jake's book, her own. It had been a good evening, quietly companionable, even though Jake had spoken little.

Clearly he didn't want to be bothered with her on a journey, and he didn't want to be held back while she walked slowly round Plymouth. He was vigorous, full of energy, even though a lot of it was bad-tempered.

What had she expected? She sat down, her face miserable. Who was he, anyway? He meant nothing to her. Most of the time he was angry, and she was only doing this to be able to stay without constant disputes. She didn't even like him, and he was a man!

Emma was feeling strangely content next day when she woke up. Jake had come back just before it was dark, and she had been all set to ignore him. She had got over her misery and was now merely annoyed at his attitude. He had walked into the sitting-room and she hadn't even turned her head.

'New books,' he had said gruffly, and before she could even look up he had tossed a whole armful of books on to the settee beside her. 'I'm getting bored with Eric's choice,' he had continued as she had looked at him in astonishment. 'I wasn't sure of your taste, so I brought a selection.'

He most certainly had. Thrillers, romance, travel books and one or two books that looked too heavy reading for Emma. She just stared at them, keeping her head down, not knowing at all what to say. After all, they weren't on the best of terms.

'I'm sorry I didn't take you,' he muttered when she said nothing. 'It occurred to me later that you might have wanted something—like talc or shampoo or... Look,' he added with growing exasperation, 'I'm an uncouth bastard at the best of times.'

He just walked out then, leaving Emma almost open-
mouthed. She imagined he wasn't used to explaining his
nasty behaviour to anyone. She should perhaps be flat-
tered, but she was not going to allow herself to be lulled
into any feeling of loneliness when he wasn't there in
future.

The evening was spent very quietly as she and Jake
delved into the new books, and she was not too self-
conscious to put her feet up on the settee and stretch
out comfortably by the fire after Mrs Teal's delicious
supper had been eaten. From time to time she found
herself looking up at Jake as he sat reading, and after
a while she was watching him more than her book. She
had to admit he intrigued her.

Her own attitude intrigued her too. More than that—
it amazed her. She had never imagined she would be
able to stay alone in a house with a man. She had not
even been really alone with Gareth ever. They had gone
out to places and sometimes he had come to the flat for
a meal, but there was always the likelihood of Sue's
coming back. With Jake, though, she could simply be
here with no anxiety. She could sleep in this isolated
house, her door unlocked, and never think of her old
fear.

In the light of the new day it all seemed a bit unreal.
She stopped brushing her hair as a thought struck her.
She was almost happy. She wasn't thinking of Gareth at
all now with anything but annoyance at his duplicity.
Jake made her happy! That irritating, cool, unpredictable man had slipped into her mind. It was more
than that, but she hastily pushed any other speculation
aside and finished brushing her hair.

'Emma?' There was a tap on the door and Jake called
to her. 'Are you awake? I've got some tea here for you.
Can I come in?'

'Just—just a minute!' The unexpected with Jake always sent her into a flurry and she made a grab for her dressing-gown, but he must have misheard her because he walked in even before she had it on. She hastily draped it round her and looked at him worriedly. Her heart had started to race alarmingly.

'I've only brought you a cup of tea,' he said rather tightly as he saw the look on her face and totally misunderstood. 'I want to get started. The light's excellent this morning.' He glanced at her as she sat on the bed, her fingers anxiously clutching the robe around her. 'I didn't expect you to be awake yet. It's early.'

'I got up early. I have been doing for a good few days. It means I can get my exercises done and then get down at the same time as you. I—I know you don't like to be kept waiting,' she added quickly.

'The exercises. Damn, I forgot about those. Sorry.'

He looked quite put out and she relaxed a bit from her tight restraint. 'It's all right. I won't be long.'

He suddenly seemed to realise he still had her cup of tea, and he walked in and put it on the dressing-table.

'I'll not be too long,' she repeated hastily as he still stood there, watching her.

It was very intimate to have him here in her room. Mrs Teal hadn't come yet, she knew, but it didn't worry her at all now. She liked to look up and see Jake. Her cheeks flooded with colour at such unexpected thoughts and he looked at her patiently, clearly thinking he was scaring her all over again.

'Did they give you the exercises at the hospital?'

'Yes. I would have known anyway. I was training to be a physiotherapist, as I told you. I will be again when I'm better,' she added forcefully, waiting for him to go.

He didn't. He just stood there, looking down at her.

'Can I watch?' he asked unexpectedly, and she gasped at the idea.

'It—it's private. I—I can't have anyone watching me.'

'Why? Don't they watch you when you go to the hospital? Doesn't this man—Skelton—watch you?'

'Sometimes, well, he used to at first, but—but he's a doctor.'

'What difference does that make?' he asked quietly. 'I've painted more nudes than you've had hot dinners. A leg isn't going to bother me.'

Emma looked at him frustratedly, almost speechless. He astounded her more often than not. She should have been terrified with him in here, but all she felt was astonishment and a sort of warm confusion.

'I don't do my exercises nude.'

'So what's the problem? Why can't I stay here with you and watch?' he asked doggedly. 'I want to.'

'Jake. Please!' She looked up at him helplessly and he looked back, his dark eyes suddenly quite sombre.

'I like looking at you,' he said abruptly. 'I don't see why I can't stay and chat to you while you do your exercises. Anyway, I'll probably want to do another portrait of you after this one. I'll be seeing plenty of you.'

'I'm not posing without...!' she began frantically, getting hastily to her feet and forgetting the dressing-gown that slid to the floor.

'Of course you're not,' he assured her softly, his eyes moving over her slender figure in the while satin nightie. 'I never suggested it, did I?'

They both heard the door slam as Mrs Teal arrived, and Jake looked at her moodily.

'Everything's quite academic now,' he pointed out. 'It's not going to be long before breakfast is ready, so we haven't got any jump-on time, after all.'

Before she could recover he had walked out, and all her resolve to do her exercises faded as she sat, feeling utterly shaken, and drank her tea. By the time she went down to breakfast she was feeling quite light-headed. It had been so unlike Jake and so unlike her too. A few weeks ago she would have been either screaming or fainting; now all she felt was warm inside.

Jake had finished and gone to the studio, and she tackled her breakfast quickly, not wanting to keep him waiting, and when she joined him he was back to his businesslike self, no smile at all. He merely glanced up at her and motioned her to the settee where she posed, behaving as if he had never seen her earlier.

'Let's get to it. We missed most of yesterday.'

Emma arranged herself as she remembered, feeling a little let down, and almost at once he strode over to move her.

'I want a slight adjustment to the pose today.' He sounded distant and cold. 'How far will that leg bend?'

'As far as I want it to,' Emma said testily. 'It's not a wooden leg!'

'Forgive me,' he derided. 'I realise that I offend. Call it an artistic quirk.'

'What do you want me to do?' Emma asked, staring at him crossly. She was terribly disappointed. She had no idea what had got into her lately. Why she had expected him to be different after this morning she didn't know. It had been just one of his many peculiarities. Maybe all famous artists were like that?

'Oh, I'll do it. You just relax into the new pose.'

His hand came to her ankle, and she tried not to stiffen as he moved her until her foot was on the settee, her leg bent up, the other stretched out.

'A slightly more voluptuous pose, I think,' he murmured, treating her like a doll. 'Now the buttons.'

This time he unfastened them, and Emma felt a trembling rush of feeling, a turbulent upheaval inside her that was not fear. His warm hand brushed her skin as he arranged the dress off her shoulder, his breath stirring the hair on her forehead, and that scent of aftershave teased her senses again. He turned his attention to the scarf, ignoring her completely, and it was only when everything was arranged that his eyes moved over her creamy skin.

It was like being touched. A weird fear raced over her that drowned the warm disturbance inside. She flinched, unable to stop the involuntary action, and he looked up at her.

'Keep calm,' he said softly, his eyes holding hers. 'Nothing has happened to you, and nothing is going to.'

His gaze locked with hers until his head was close, and then his lips covered her own quickly. He never touched her at all. There was just the slow drowsy movement of his mouth against hers, and she was so unprepared for the kiss that she offered no resistance. Everything inside her relaxed, her head moving to the high back of the settee as the pressure of his lips stayed insistently against her own, coaxing and warm.

She was dazed as he lifted his head and looked down at her, and a smile played across his firm mouth.

'Stay just like that,' he murmured. 'That's exactly what I want.'

Jake was back behind the easel before it dawned on her that he had done it deliberately to get the pose he was seeking, and shame mixed with real anger. She raised her head and looked at him stonily.

'You did very well to call yourself uncouth!' she snapped. 'Is that how you arrange all the poses? Do you kiss all your models until they get into the mood you want?'

It was a very unwise thing to say and Jake never even bothered to look up; his eyes were following the swift movement of his hands.

'I only kiss my models if they need it,' he assured her, adding quietly, 'or if I do.'

She knew he didn't need it as far as she was concerned; therefore he must have thought she needed it. For the rest of the session she was silent and stiff, shame dulling every other feeling, and he kept her hard at it too, only easing off when it became apparent that she was really hurting. He only noticed that when Mrs Teal called from the door that lunch would be ready in twenty minutes.

He wiped his brush and strode to the door.

'Hold it for half an hour, Mrs Teal,' he shouted. 'Emma needs to unwind a bit. I kept her too long this time.'

'Is she all right?' Mrs Teal came bustling along and Emma managed to get her dress fastened and present a more demure image before the housekeeper confronted her with anxious eyes.

'I'm just stiff, that's all,' Emma assured her. She limped into the hall. 'I think I'll have a quick walk.'

'You'd be better off with a warm bath,' Jake said, his eyes on her leg and the slightly pale look of her face. 'I kept you too long. Why the hell didn't you say it was hurting you?'

Mrs Teal looked on worriedly, and Emma could have killed Jake. She was not yet recovered from her own thoughts that she must be decent before Mrs Teal came into the studio. If she wasn't decent then what was she doing letting Jake see her like that? Now he seemed to think he could blame her for his own thoughtlessness.

'I know what I need,' she muttered, collecting her coat and stepping out of the door before he could make any further comment.

The moment the door was closed between them she relaxed, her mind teasing away at her astonishing change of attitude. How was it that she could let Jake touch her, kiss her, even be close to her at all? He was nor-

mally hateful, and she would normally have run a mile
to avoid a man like that, or any man.

It could be that being cooped up with him in this
barren place was affecting her. Then again, she wasn't
now as self-conscious about her leg, and that was almost
entirely due to his attitude. Truth to tell, he had her in
a turmoil most of the time. She knew he was filled with
masculine aggression and she was only safe from his acid
tongue because he needed her for the portrait, but something was happening inside her that had never happened
before, feelings that were new to her.

She was too distant in her thoughts to be really aware
of her surroundings, and as a hand came to her arm she
jumped and spun round, fear instantly in her eyes.

'It's only me!' Jake looked hostile, his grip tightening. 'God knows why you take off by yourself when
you're as jumpy as a cat.'

She stood still, staring at him, and he turned her back
to the path, every movement of his body a rebuke.

'You wanted to walk. Let's get to it!'

He irritated her so much when he was like this. She
wanted to order him back to the house. It was nothing
to do with Jake what she did. If she reacted badly,
though, he would only snap at her, and she didn't quite
feel up to any argument with him. She was too busy
assessing her own attitude. She went on silently but
snatched her arm away and walked by herself.

'I'm not going far.' She knew it sounded sullen but
there was nothing she could do to keep the sound out
of her voice. She felt vulnerable with him now, scared
for quite a new reason. 'I really didn't need company.'

'Maybe I did,' he muttered, easily keeping pace with
her. 'Working with you is somewhat of a strain.'

'It was your idea in the first place,' Emma reminded
him sharply. 'Let's call the whole thing a mistake and

forget it.' He was trying to hurt her again and she knew he could now.

'No way! This is the best thing I've ever done.'

She glanced at his set face secretly, her long lashes hiding her eyes.

'You can't possibly mean that.'

He made no move to answer, and there was an austere look about his face that made her doubt his words anyway. If it had been so good he would have been pleased. He didn't look pleased.

'Is it good, Jake?' She badly wanted to know, a feeling of frustration growing as he still walked on as if she had said nothing. 'Jake!' She stopped by an outcrop of rock and held on to his sleeve, stopping him too. 'Jake, why are you ignoring me? Is the portrait good?'

The speed of his reaction this time left her scared.

'Yes, it's good!' He faced her abruptly, his hands against her shoulders. 'I've already said it's the best thing I've ever done. What more do you want me to say?' He sounded so hostile that she moved away, only to find herself backed up against the rock.

'If—if it's good then why are you so angry?'

He glared at her for a second and then came closer, his hand once more on her shoulders, pressing her back against the rock.

'Angry?' he muttered, his eyes moving over the pallor of her skin, the soft tremble of her lips. 'Do you think it pleases me to have to look at you all day? If you hadn't come I would never have thought of the portrait. Normally my models come and go, all under their own steam. I'm not faced with them at breakfast, lunch and dinner. I'm not aware that they're asleep in the same house. I don't have to care for them, guard them!'

She winced, shrinking further away, colour flaring over her skin. He felt the need to be there, taking care of her, sure that she was too lame and incompetent to survive alone. Nobody had made her feel so useless. Tears glazed her eyes and she turned her head aside to escape from the censure in his harsh gaze.

'I—I don't need guarding,' she whispered. 'I don't need anyone.'

'Emma?'

He moved closer, his body cutting off the bite of the wind, and she dropped her head, the only way she could avoid his eyes with any safety.

'Emma!' There was a curious rough sound to his voice and his hand came to her face, lifting it. 'I have to stay close. If I don't you'll run out on me, won't you? Won't you?' he insisted when she refused to open her eyes and looked back at him.

She couldn't trust herself to answer. It was astonishing how he could hurt her; a stray tear escaped from her tightly closed eyes and his hand came to her silky head, his fingers toying with the dark strands of shining hair.

'Why is it that I can't come right out and say what I mean with you?' he mused.

It had her opening her eyes and he looked at her intently, a bitter twist to his mouth when he saw the swimming tears.

'I hurt you,' he said softly. 'You think... Hell! I don't care if you're lame. Don't go imagining that, Emma!' He sounded harsh again and she twisted her face away, but this time he would not allow it. Both hands came to capture her head, his fingers spearing into her hair as he lifted her face, his mouth on hers before she could utter a sound.

It wasn't like the kiss in the studio. It wasn't gentle either. It was all frustrated masculinity, but even so it didn't frighten her. He just took possession of her mouth, getting a startled response that was all inexperience and surprise. She was defenceless against the searching pressure, shaken when he plundered her sweetness for endless seconds.

A breathless, bewildering feeling seemed to overcome her, a curious bitter pain knotting her stomach, and she was still paralysed by her own reaction when he lifted his head and looked at her with strange burning eyes.

'That's why I don't want to look at you each day, why I don't want you to be sleeping in the same house,' he said thickly, his head sinking to her silken hair. His teeth tugged sensually at her earlobe, his words murmured against her ear. 'Your leg doesn't bother me. It's every inch of you that bothers me!'

She was still numb, still fighting her own inexperienced reaction to passion, and he drew her hard against him, urging her head to his shoulder, his hand sliding inside the heavy wool of her coat to her waist. She could feel the warmth of his fingers, feel their restless probing, the way his thumb moved against the base of her ribcage, and the old fear came with a wild rush.

'*No!*'

Her paralysed limbs surged into life, her hands frantically beating him away, even though they shook uncontrollably.

'Go away! Leave me alone!' She could hear her own voice almost screaming, and she could see his face, white and shocked.

'Emma! I never meant to...'

He reached out his hand, but her eyes were wide and terrified, pushing him away as she fainted.

'Emma?' Jake's voice was a million miles away as she came round. Her eyes were wide open in fear at once, and he knelt by her as she lay on the grass near the rock, crouching beside her, his own face pale as she raised her hand to her mouth. 'Dear God! I'm not going to hurt you! I'm not even going to touch you!'

Apparently he changed his mind about that almost at once because he reached for her and lifted her to her feet. 'Let's get you back out of this cold wind.' He sounded cool, matter-of-fact, distant, and his return to his old ways helped in some measure to restore her. 'Can you walk back?'

She just nodded, and moved with him when he began to go back to the house. They had been close all the time, the side of the house was still not far off, and she came slowly to her senses, shame flooding through her.

'Jake,' she began huskily, but he shook his head irritably.

'No!' he grated. 'I've got to come to terms with this. Just leave it!'

It was a very subdued meal. Emma dragged her way back to normality, at least a kind of normality. She was ashamed as she had never been before, unable to meet Jake's eyes, not that he had had any desire to even look at her. And Mrs Teal watched them both surreptitiously, well aware that something was wrong, her face worried. She lingered a lot later too, as if she was afraid to leave them alone together, and Jake noticed that with tightened lips.

It only increased the burden of Emma's guilt. Her reaction to him had been automatic, she had given no thought to it. Her mind had sensed threat and overruled her body's delight.

Jake made no attempt to resume the painting and after a while she heard him leave the house, his car sounding viciously angry too, the way he was driving it. She had managed to make him feel guilty and it had been nothing to do with Jake at all really. It was her own private nightmare, something she could not control. She had also made Mrs Teal suspicious of Jake.

She lingered in the kitchen and then walked miserably into the sitting-room, and it was there that Mrs Teal

found her as she at last admitted to herself that she would
have to go home and get her own house seen to.

'I'll have to go,' she said worriedly, standing and
looking at Emma's pale face. 'My husband will be in
soon and there's nothing ready for him. Will you be all
right?'

'Of course. I always am.' Emma smiled at her, but it
did little to drive the suspicion from the round and kindly
face.

'I thought...' She couldn't bring herself to say anything, and Emma blushed and looked down; better to
tell a small lie and get this over than to have Jake blamed
for nothing at all.

'I'm a bit embarrassed, that's all, and I think Mr
Garrani is too,' she said. 'I—I was too stiff. I shouldn't
have gone out. The pain was bad and I fainted. He had
to look after me and, after all, I'm nothing to him and
he's so famous. I felt like a fool. It was awful!'

'Is that all?' Mrs Teal's face creased in smiles.
'Heavens, love, he's a grown man, not a boy. I should
think he's seen a woman faint before with less reason.'
She shook her head in amusement and prepared to leave
with a great deal more willingness. 'It won't have
bothered him at all. It's your shyness. Just talk normally
to him and it will all go away. He's probably forgotten
it by now.'

She went off happily and Emma sank to the settee
with a sigh of frustration. He wouldn't have forgotten
it by now. He wouldn't be likely to forget that she had
had a hysterical fit. That embarrassment would live with
them both, and the sooner she went, the better.

She admitted to herself that even if she had had a flat
of her own she didn't want to go. In some strange way
she needed Jake. Leaving would be like a self-inflicted
pain, and she couldn't even leave easily. They had both

ignored the fact that her car was standing outside in the same condition it had been in when she had arrived here.

She limped to the window and looked outside. The fog was there but it was only thin, and she suddenly remembered she had to go to London tomorrow to see Mr Skelton. Her life had changed so much here that the appointment had completely slipped her mind.

When Jake came in later she was sitting staring into the fire, and she forced herself to look up at him.

'I—I'm sorry, Jake.' It was little enough to say but it was all she could manage.

'Think nothing of it.' He was cold and unapproachable, but she had to approach him. She stood and looked at him, and this time he was the one avoiding her eyes.

'Tomorrow I have to go to London,' she blurted out, anxious to get all the rage out of the way before her courage ran down.

It stopped him as he was going out of the door, and he came back, not very far, clearly expecting another outburst of insanity if he even came near.

'You're running back, then?' he asked bitterly. 'You're so terrified of me that you're on the run again? I thought you'd given the flat up because a creep had moved in with your flatmate?'

'I'm not running away,' she said steadily. 'I have to see Mr Skelton.'

'Your father confessor?' he asked tightly.

'He's an orthopaedic surgeon. He operated on my leg. I have an appointment and I forgot all about it,' she said miserably.

He stood perfectly still and looked at her for a long time.

'Then what?'

'I'm coming back here.' She couldn't meet his gaze and looked down at her feet. 'Can I come back, Jake?'

'It's not my house!' he bit out. 'In point of fact, you have more right to be here than I have.'

'If you're angry because Mrs Teals thinks... I told her I fainted and that it had embarrassed you.'

She looked up at him and he was obviously shocked, his black eyebrows raised in disbelief.

'Why the hell did you do that? I don't care what Mrs Teal thinks.'

'She was suspicious and worried, and I didn't think it fair that you should be blamed for my—my hysteria. She seemed to be imagining that—that...'

His lips twisted in a smile of near derision, but he looked a lot less angry. 'I can't make my mind up whether I want her to think I'm embarrassed by seeing a woman faint, or whether I want her to think I was attacking you,' he murmured wryly. 'I'll give it some thought; either way I lose. I'm either a villain or an idiot.'

He walked over to her and looked down at her.

'I could do with a break from this fog-bound house. I'll drive you up to London. What time is this appointment?'

'It's in the afternoon, but you don't have to...'

'You're afraid to be with me?' he began frustratedly, and she put her hand rather timidly on his arm.

'No. It was nothing at all to do with you, Jake. I couldn't help it.' His hand covered hers and she felt warm at once. 'I don't mind you—you touching me, Jake. I didn't think you were going to... I can't help it. It happens.'

'Has it ever happened so badly?'

She shook her head and avoided his eyes. 'No. Nobody has ever been so close to me...except...I mean...'

He looked at her for a minute and then turned away. 'I know what you mean. I'll make some tea,' he remarked, over his shoulder as usual. 'I can see it's going to be one of those afternoons.'

Emma sank back to the settee, her face flushed with pleasure. By some small miracle she had managed to get him back to his normal ways and, even though they were sardonic and cool ways, they suited her. She was used to him, safe with him. Her panic had drained away, and she was only left with her first reaction to his kiss. Now that she dared to think about it the same unbelievable joy came back. The journey to London seemed like a thrilling ride to wonderland. If only...

When he came back in she forced herself to take the initiative, getting the tray from him and serving them both, and after a quick glance at her he picked up his book. She was happy that he didn't want to go out of the room, and she settled down with her own book, snuggling back into the strange contentment that being with Jake brought.

'Emma.' His voice had her looking up a few seconds later, and he was watching her, not reading at all. 'Will you tell me about it?'

'No. I can't.'

'Does Skelton know?'

'He's not a psychiatrist.'

'I wasn't suggesting you needed one. Things are better when they're talked out, though. Have you ever told anyone? Your father?' he added when she shook her head.

'Oh, no! He had enough to cope with.'

'Tell me, then. I'm a stranger. Even if you decide to stay here permanently, I shall be going. You'll never see me again then. A passing stranger—what better way to get things out into the open?'

'I can't.' The thought of his going, of her never seeing him again was suddenly more real than any nightmare, any past terror. She was silent, unable to look at him in case he saw her sudden despair, and he sighed.

'Never mind, then. At least I know not to touch you.'

'It wasn't that,' she said urgently, looking up. 'I told you, I don't mind you touching me. I'm not at all afraid of you.'

'All the same, I think we'll not get around to any nude poses,' he mocked softly.

She raised her chin and looked at him defiantly.

'It wouldn't bother me.'

He didn't answer, and when she looked up again he was still watching her, a smile playing around his lips, and his eyes were warm for the first time ever, really warm.

'Whether it was meant as one or not, I take that as a compliment,' he said quietly.

CHAPTER SIX

To EMMA'S surprise, Mr Skelton was pleased.

'Remarkable change in two weeks,' he said as she sat facing him after her examination. 'All for the better too.'

'You mean my leg's improved?' She hadn't really done anything to improve it, as far as she could see, except to do the exercises fairly thoroughly.

'Well, it's no worse, but that's not entirely what I meant. You've changed, Miss Shaw. I can see it myself. There's a certain air about you that wasn't there before and, as I say, it seems to me it's for the better, whatever has brought it about.'

Jake, Emma thought. She was happy. That was the difference. It was impossible to describe her feelings for Jake. She had never felt like this in her whole life. He was exciting. He was utterly self-sufficient, almost secret, and his dark good looks were even partially alarming, but when he was there a certain difference was in the air, almost a magic.

Her panic at his passionate kisses had faded as if it had never been there. There was no lingering shame. Jake had not allowed it. He had talked to her on the way as if nothing had happened at all, and last night had helped, the way he had accepted things. Emma also accepted them. She had come to realise that her fright, her attacks of panic were a deep-rooted fear that now should have gone. It was a matter of conquering it and before she had met Jake she had made no attempt to even begin to become rehabilitated.

Posing had changed her too and so had the odd thing he had said as he worked. Slowly she was beginning to be aware of herself as a woman, and who had done that but Jake? He had not done it deliberately. It seemed to be his very presence that challenged her to be female. If only... Her face flushed like a rose, and Mr Skelton's eyes twinkled pale blue behind his spectacles.

'There is the odd thing that can give a person a new driving force,' he said with a small smile. 'It's always good. It helps with any healing, urges one on. Keep it up, Miss Shaw. I think we can make your next appointment for a month now.'

Emma walked out with a smile on her face, and Jake put down his newspaper as she came to the car and slid inside confidently.

'You're looking better,' he murmured. 'Skelton must have something special.'

'He told me I was different,' Emma said with a smile. 'He was very pleased. I don't have to go again for four weeks. It's the longest gap I've had.'

'Apart from the fact that you look different,' Jake said drily, 'what's the situation about your leg?'

'He seemed quite pleased. It's not any worse.' She looked across at him. 'You said it didn't matter.'

She wanted Jake to tell her again. What Jake thought now seemed to be the most important thing in life.

'It doesn't matter to me,' he informed her quietly. 'It matters to you, though.'

'Not as much as it did. I—I feel more normal somehow...'

'Normal enough to stay up in London for the night and go out somewhere?' he enquired in a careful voice.

It scared her instantly, and her hands clenched without any chance of stopping them. There it was again, the automatic reaction. Self-defence for no reason other than the past. He waited, saying nothing, not even looking at her, and Emma stifled the rising fear before it could take hold of her.

'If you like.'

'Surely it's if *you* like?' he pointed out, adding nothing further. He went on looking straight ahead.

She felt quite ridiculous making such a fuss, even if it was a silent fuss. If she didn't have courage with Jake she never would have courage.

'I'm not really dressed for going out.'

He looked across at her, his eyes running over her soft woollen suit. It was deep blue, almost the colour of her eyes; her shoes were dainty with a sensible heel, comfortable to walk in. Her jacket was on the back seat.

'You look fine to me. I'm not exactly dressed for the Ritz, so we won't go there.'

Jake had come out in dark trousers and a black denim shirt. It was open at the neck, showing a strong brown throat. His jacket was with hers in the back of the car. She looked hastily away from the masculine power that had recently begun to fascinate her.

'You look nice. You always do. It's different for you, though, isn't it?'

'Why?' He sounded quietly intrigued, and she glanced up, meeting his eyes.

'Well, you're strong, famous, people expect you to look as you do.'

He suddenly laughed, his head thrown back, the first time he had ever really shown such outright amusement.

'Strong and famous! I haven't the faintest idea what that means, you obscure creature.' He smiled across at her, his humour just controlled. 'Listen, I know quite a few people who are even more odd than you. Believe me, with them you'll be dressed to kill.'

'Are they artists?'

'Yes. Fame hasn't made me give up the people who are still struggling. I struggled right along with them once. I know how to rough it. Care to chance it?'

'All right.' She made up her mind. She had never done anything without planning before, and if she was really going to live then she must take chances. 'Where will we stay?'

'I've got a flat here. It's in a pretty down-market area, but when I first got it I thought it was paradise, so I've kept it. There's only one bedroom, but there's a nice long settee where people stay from time to time. I'll sleep there.'

Emma just sat and looked at him, and he leaned across to tilt her face.

'We're alone every night at Credlestone Hall,' he pointed out quietly. 'Not a soul for miles. This flat is in the middle of a bustling metropolis that rarely sleeps. What's the difference, except to your advantage?'

'I—I didn't mean to be suspicious. I never thought...'

'So do we stay?' he asked good-humouredly, pushing aside her worries, and she nodded, smiling, accepting the excitement that Jake brought.

'Yes.'

'Right, then. Let's get a meal and then a freshen up at the flat. It's already almost six o'clock. I know a place where the parties start at seven and go on until seven the next morning.'

Inside she was in a turmoil, but this time it was not fear. Jake wanted to take her out, to keep her with him. He could easily have come to London at any time and left her behind, but he was asking her to share something for the first time ever, and she was gloriously happy.

The flat really was in a run-down area, but nobody seemed to be annoyed at the sight of Jake's expensive car. It was almost dark but there were plenty of people hanging around talking in the street, and many of them waved cheerfully to Jake, calling out to him and getting the same witty chatter back.

Emma felt a little lost. Jake came from another world, a world where normal rules didn't seem to apply. It was testing her nerve greatly, and she wondered if Jake knew that. Many of the people seemed to be young, students, long-haired and oddly dressed, and Jake went into one of the flats at the impassioned invitation of two of them.

'How is it, Jake?' The young man stood back as he uncovered a picture on canvas. 'It's only half done. Is it worth finishing?'

Emma stood and watched, feeling almost as anxious as they did. The young man was watching Jake with an almost pleading look, his girlfriend biting her nails.

'Suppose I said it wasn't?' Jake murmured after a minute, his eyes still on the glowing colours.

'I suppose I'd finish it and then maybe paint over it. I can't afford to have useless canvas lying around.'

'Paint over it and I'll flatten you,' Jake growled. 'It's brilliant!'

'Jake! You mean it?' The young man actually went pale, and Emma realised that she too had been holding her breath, waiting for the word of the master.

'How many times have I pulled your work to pieces?' Jake snapped. 'What makes you think I've softened any?'

The young man started grinning, and Jake slapped him on the back.

'This is it, man,' he laughed, and the girl flung her arms round Jake's neck, hugging him. He slapped her familiarly on the bottom and the smile died on Emma's face as a feeling shot through her she had never felt before. She turned to the door, and almost at once Jake was beside her, stepping out into the street.

'What's the matter? Did they scare you?'

'Of course not.' She couldn't look at him right now, and he led her across the road as she fought to be normal.

'You disapproved, then?'

'No!'

He never asked any more questions, and Emma fought down dismay. She didn't want Jake to touch anyone else, even though he had hardly ever touched her and even though when he did she panicked. She wanted to shout at him, shake him. The intensity of the feeling was painful and she could only keep quiet. Without even knowing it, she had begun to think that Jake belonged to her.

The flat looked like the other from the outside but when he opened the door she gave a little gasp. It was beautifully and expensively furnished, much more expensively than her uncle's house. The settee in question was long and white, bright cushions on it. The carpet was almost white too, and the whole place seemed to be dotted with antiques, carefully chosen to add even more beauty to the room.

He drew the curtains and turned to look at her.

'Once you're inside,' he explained, 'it's quite easy to forget the edge of poverty that artists here live on.'

'Do you help them?' she asked a bit breathlessly. This place was part of a Jake she didn't know. At Credlestone Hall and since then she had quite forgotten that he was wealthy, that his work was in great demand and that his grudgingly done portraits brought in thousands and more.

'The artists in the street? Sometimes. Not too often, though, only when they're desperate. Fat living takes the edge off things when you're young.'

'Did it with you?' she asked wryly, her eyes on the expensive furniture.

'It didn't get the chance. I never lived fat. I was as poor as they come. It adds a sort of vicious energy to things. The drive to succeed is almost a drive to stay alive. It sharpens the eye.'

He glanced at her rather impatiently, still puzzled, it seemed, by her reaction of a few minutes ago, and she knew she had been sharp and walked out of that other flat almost rudely. It wasn't something she could start explaining to Jake.

'The bathroom is in there, by the bedroom. If you want a quick freshen-up I'll be sorting out the bedding for you for tonight.'

'I could sleep on the settee,' she offered.

'Just because I don't pour wealth on to artists who would be irritated by such benevolence doesn't mean that I'd sleep in bed and leave a lady to occupy the settee,' he informed her sourly.

'I'm sure that what you do is none of my business!' Emma snapped, her mind seeing again his familiarity with that girl, a sort of trembling hurt inside her.

'I'm sure too,' he muttered as she walked off to have a quick freshen-up, not at all sure now if she should have stayed and not wanting to see Jake so intimately friendly with anyone else. If it was a party for artists, how would he behave there? How would she be expected to behave?

'If there's dancing then I won't be able to join in,' she said as she walked back later, her hair brushed to a dark shine, her lips softly pink.

'Believe me, it's going to be so crowded that you'll be lucky to even stand,' he mocked. 'I've been on the phone and they're expecting us. Let's go.'

'Maybe they won't like me?' Emma felt a surge of nerves now, his attitude making her feel alone.

'They'll never notice you,' he derided. 'I'm the one who's expected with bated breath. Fame follows me. The

celebrity is with you. Do you notice who's with a film
star, unless you're jealous?'

The words were meant to deflate her and they did.
The feeling sent her into a deep silence that lasted until
they got to the party. She was worried that if she spoke
Jake would somehow get a clue about how she felt.
Living in the isolation of Credlestone Hall had made
two weeks' acquaintance seem like a lifetime. It had
become easier each day to think that Jake was a sort of
private possession. Now the thought was firmly knocked
out of her mind. Maybe he knew, maybe that was why
he had suggested staying all night in London?

He hadn't changed, although she was sure he would
have had extra clothes at his flat. He hadn't put his jacket
on either. The cuffs of the black denim shirt were turned
back, a square gold watch drawing her eyes to the
strength of his wrists, the grace of those hands. She felt
oddly breathless, a little desperate, much too aware that
Jake was beside her. She had never felt like that before,
never simply wanted to keep him to herself.

Emma was surprised to find the house quite big.
Somehow she had expected another flat, impoverished
artists crowded into it. She mentioned this thought, and
Jake scowled sullenly.

'Not all artists are poverty-stricken. There's nothing
about me that suggest the pauper. If there is then I assure
you it's erroneous.'

The sharpness of his words left her miserable. He was
tired of her silence, and now that he was back to civi-
lisation he was once again aware that she was an oddity.
Emma didn't need anyone to tell her she would not be
the life and soul of the party. And he didn't explain anything to her either—it was another man who did that.

In spite of the size of the house, it was crowded to the walls, music playing, people dancing, and noise such as she had never heard in a house.

'You're with Jake?' An older man came up to her and handed her a drink. Jake had been swept away as soon as they had arrived.

'I'm supposed to be.'

He heard the anxiety in her voice and laughed.

'He'll find you. It's always the same here on party nights. Did he tell you he used to live here?'

She shook her head and he smiled, looking at the crowded room.

'It doesn't always look like this, only for a party. Normally ten to twelve people live and work here. It was bought as a sort of commune, and Jake was here once, before he got his own flat, before he made it big, of course,' he added with a smile. 'The whole thing works well. Everybody knows everybody else. They borrow from each other.'

'Do you live here?' Emma had noticed that not everyone was young; in fact, there were people of all ages here.

'Not now. I used to be here but, like Jake, I made it, though not to Jake's standard.' He looked across at Jake. 'He's brilliant, mind you. Always was.'

Emma's eyes followed his. Jake was across the room, talking to a group of people, and their eyes held for a minute. He seemed to watch her intently, and her breath felt as if it was caught in her throat. She didn't want him to look away but he did. A woman came up and slid her arm into his, he smiled down at her, and the next thing Emma saw was the way he danced with her, his attention now given to the woman as if Emma didn't exist at all.

More people arrived, but it did nothing to take Emma's mind off Jake. He seemed to go from one partner to another, his face smiling, his eyes on each new woman as if she were the only one in the world. She had never heard his name spoken so much either.

'Jake, darling!' It seemed that everyone there was queuing up to be held in those arms, and Emma made herself look away, knowing it was hurting her. She was grateful when someone else came to talk and take her mind from him. They were so familiar with him and she felt bereft. She didn't really know Jake at all. She was just some chance acquaintance to him.

'What are you drinking?' A young man with long fair hair came up and sat beside her.

'As little as possible.' She grinned at him, determined to show that she too could capture attention.

'I know. It's easy enough at a do like this to keep on drinking and not even notice it,' he agreed, adding with an interested look at her, 'You're Jake's girl, then?'

'I came with Jake, yes.'

'Sorry. Is it a touchy subject? Had words, have you? I can see he's dancing with just about everyone else.'

She didn't much feel like pointing out that Jake could hardly dance with her. She hadn't moved since she had come in here, so nobody had noticed her limp. She didn't need to be reminded, either, that Jake was dancing with everyone. Seeing his arms go round another woman was like a sharply stabbing pain. He seemed to hold some of them much too close, and he was certainly enjoying it.

'Haven't upset you, have I?' The young man leaned across closely, and she forced a smile.

'Of course not.'

When she looked up Jake was towering over them both, a look in his eyes that scared her. He looked almost dangerous.

'How are things?' He nodded to the young man and then reached out, drawing Emma to her feet. 'It's dance time,' he growled.

'You know I can't. Don't make me look a fool, Jake, *please*!' she whispered to him urgently as they moved away, and he drew her tightly against him, both arms around her, sheltering her from people who brushed past, and her hands came uncertainly to his chest.

'Cruelty isn't my particular speciality,' he admonished. 'Look around,' he added in a low voice. 'If you can see anybody's feet I'll give you a pound. In this crowd nobody would notice if we fell down until they stepped on us.'

It was true. They were hardly moving. It was just a mass of people circling and it looked as if for most of them this was merely an excuse to be close.

'I'm sorry,' Emma muttered miserably. She knew he had only come back for her because he felt guilty at her being alone when he had brought her here. Why he was bothering with her she didn't know. Jake didn't need her as she needed him.

He pulled her closer, his face against her hair.

'Were you beginning to feel neglected?' he murmured against her ear.

'No. I had a few companions.' She tried not to shiver but it was an impossible task. Everything that Jake did sent shock waves through her now.

'I noticed. All of them men, too.'

'The women were all too busy dancing with you,' she rejoined tartly before she could stop herself. She felt like a shrew at once, and he drew back to look down at her.

'As we seem to have been watching each other's activities all the time, it would appear to be a bit pointless to separate,' he suggested quietly, his arms tightening as he moved her back to the strength of his body.

It would have been easy to just sink against him, but she held herself stiffly and resisted the urge to follow her instincts. It wasn't nice to feel the jealousy that still flashed through her, and she was sure he hadn't been watching her activities. She was the one who had been watching, every glance a small torture. Jake had made it fairly plain that she was just another woman here, an uninteresting one too. Her eyes misted over and she turned her head sideways in case he saw.

His hand lifted and moved to her hair, coming beneath the silken weight of it to move soothingly against her nape, his fingers warm.

'What's the matter, then?' He sounded huskily gentle, as if he was sorry for her, and she didn't want that at all but it melted her bewildered pain. It was her undoing. She did what she wanted so badly to do and moved willingly closer, accepting the insistent pressure of his arms.

'Is that better?' His voice was low against her hair and his lips brushed over the shell of her ear, his teeth nipping at her lobe for a second.

A little sound escaped from her lips and he tightened her further against him, his legs against hers.

'Don't panic on me, Emma.' His words were breathed against her skin, his lips moving lightly along her jawline, and she forgot the other people around them. They probably didn't notice, but even if they did it didn't seem to matter any more. Warmth was growing inside, a welcome feeling that she wanted after such a long time of cold fear. She wanted to throw her arms around Jake.

'You smell good, you taste good,' he murmured, his lips moving beneath her hair to her warm neck. 'It's wonderful—tasting you.'

His voice was deep and heavy, almost as if he was finding it difficult to speak at all, and she felt a sort of drowsy warmth inside that made her legs weak.

'Jake!' It wasn't much more than a trembling whisper, but he heard the soft desperation and he must have felt her shaking in his arms. He turned her to the door.

'Let's get out of this crush,' he muttered as he pushed his way to the door, his arm protecting her, side-stepping people who tried to stop him.

Outside the room Jake guided Emma along a passage, his hand tightly holding hers.

'Where—where are we going?' She was trembling almost too much to speak normally, waves of feeling flooding through her, her limp, her fright all forgotten as the warmth of Jake's hand enclosed hers. She could feel an urgency radiating from him and it seemed to match the feelings she had inside her. She badly wanted to be alone with Jake.

'I know this place. I used to live here.' He led her to a door at the end of the passage, opening it and switching on the light. 'Everyone stores their things here,' he explained gruffly. 'It's full of canvas, paints, thinners. It's a regular fire hazard but we'll run if we see a spark.'

Emma looked around and saw all the things he had mentioned. Everyone in the house seemed to have stacked things up in here. There was hardly a yard of floor space.

'It smells nice,' she offered shakily, avoiding looking at Jake. 'An exciting smell.'

'If you say so.'

He closed the door and leaned against it, just watching her intently, and she looked up at him with bewildered eyes, wondering why she wasn't scared, why she didn't feel trapped. His eyes seemed to be burning her, and she stood there helplessly, wanting him to hold her again, her skin reacting to the excitement that flooded through her. Colour flared across her cheeks, and he muttered beneath his breath, 'You know I can't go any longer without touching you, don't you?'

He reached out and pulled her against him, his arms enfolding her carefully as if he expected a panic-stricken reaction.

'Don't you?' he asked thickly as his head bent and his lips trailed kisses over her neck.

Jealousy had driven her almost to the point of tears since they had first come, and she felt a wave of almost furious joy that she was the one Jake had wanted to be alone with. She didn't know what to do but she wanted him to know it was all right. Her arms wound around his waist and she moved closer, gasping as he tightened her fiercely against him.

'You're safe, safe,' he murmured against her skin, mistaking her gasp of pleasure for fear. 'I couldn't hurt you. You've got to know that by now. Don't be frightened, Emma.'

His hand grasped her hair as he forced her head back, capturing her lips as she looked up, murmuring against her mouth until she opened it and accepted the possession of his kiss.

Nothing had prepared her for the storm of feeling that hit her then. It was almost like a searing pain that raced over all of her from her toes to her head. Before he had taken her by surprise, but this time she had known, had even hoped. This time, too, she had felt jealousy. It all contributed to her own downfall. Immediately she wanted more and more of Jake, her mind in a turmoil. She seemed to be cut off from everything, sinking deeper and deeper into delight. She could feel his body moving restlessly, his hands tightening, and it only added to the excitement that held her in a shattering grip.

His lips never left hers and she could scarcely breathe, a wild feeling of joy adding to every other excitement.

'Jake!' She tore her mouth away, but he was too committed to let her escape for long.

'Come back to me. Don't be frightened. Let me have you just for this minute, Emma. I need you!'

His hand cupped her silken head, his lips urgently seeking hers, and she came back to him almost wildly, shocked and excited when his other hand moved down her back to cup her small tight rear and hold her against him.

Her sheltered mind told her that she was being wicked to accept this, but his powerful arousal only added to her own excitement and she softened against him, her arms tightening around his neck, her heart pounding against his as he held her urgently close, every fibre of him demanding, his lips plundering her mouth.

Her soft acquiescence drove him further, his lips trailing over her throat, his demanding hands holding her against him, and her fingers moved into the thick darkness of his hair, her mouth open beneath his as he captured her lips again.

She was being devoured, drowning, innocently moving where he led, and it was Jake who pulled away, his dark head lifting, a deep groan in his throat.

'Dear God!' His breathing was ragged. 'As a fit of madness, this just about takes first prize!' he said hoarsely, moving her away as he leaned back against the door, standing for a second with his eyes closed, his chest heaving with the effort to control his feelings. 'It must be something about oil paint,' he added with shaken humour. 'Any other time and you would have been screaming or fainting.'

It dashed a cool cloud over her own racing feelings and she turned away abruptly, shocked by his immediate return to disparagement, her legs trembling so much that she swayed, her whole body aching. He must think she was a terrible person. She had never been in any situation like that before and she didn't know how she should have reacted. She had just followed her instincts and her heart.

'Emma?' His arm came around her, drawing her forward even though she was stiff with shame.

'I'm sorry!' she managed, surprised that her burning lips would even form words.

'Sorry?' He tilted her face and forced her to meet his eyes. 'Will you stop saying that?' he asked huskily. 'Who brought you here? Who kissed you? Who was desperate? I didn't give you much choice.' He looked down at her steadily, his face still tight with feeling, a blaze still deep in his eyes. His fingers trailed over her cheeks, almost tenderly caressing. 'You didn't panic, Emma. What did you feel?'

'Wicked!' She looked away and he began to laugh softly, his feelings evidently controlled now.

'Did you, though?' he mocked. 'If you were wicked, don't even think about what I was.'

He opened the door, and whether she was ready or not she had to move out into the passage.

'Want to go?' he asked quietly.

She nodded, avoiding his eyes. 'But I don't want to spoil your evening.'

'Oh, you haven't done that,' he taunted softly, making colour flood into her face. 'You nearly blew my mind, though. I think it's a good idea to go because you're not dancing with anyone else tonight. They'd be really shocked if I took them apart.'

The panic she should have felt earlier began to hit her as they drove back to Jake's flat. It kept her silent, and Jake too seemed to have sunk into a morose mood. There was no party spirit left as he opened the door of his flat and locked it against the night.

'Do you want any coffee or anything?' he asked as they went into the sitting-room.

'No. I—I just want to get to bed. It's been quite a tiring day.'

It wasn't meant as any sort of reprimand, but he took it as such.

'Yes. I quite forgot that it tires you to travel. I should never have taken you there.'

His voice was tight again and she felt miserably let down. She had never even thought it was any fault of Jake's. She went to the bedroom as he motioned her forward, and he pointed to the clean sheets for the bed.

'Can you manage or shall I do it for you?' he asked as she put her things down and turned to start.

'Jake, I'm not an invalid!' Her voice was sharp. She felt less than a woman when he fussed over her like this. It made him seem further away from her, as if she were no match whatever for his superb strength. He just turned and walked out, closing the door behind him, accepting that she was back to what he considered to be normal for her. Any tiny thing that had been between them was gone as if it had never been, and she had to do some accepting too. She had to accept that Jake was just a man, after all, and she had been more than willing to go into his arms. Anything more was impossible, even with Jake, and she realised that he knew it.

It took hardly any time at all to make the bed up, and she was standing rather forlornly, just looking at it, when Jake knocked on the door.

'I have to have a quick shower,' he pointed out quietly when she called for him to come in. 'I'll need my robe.'

Emma just nodded and looked away as he opened the wardrobe and found his robe. She couldn't seem to bring herself even to speak to him. The party and the way she had been was right at the top of her mind.

'Do you really want to go to bed right now?' He was just behind her, his hand coming to her shoulder, and she nodded, her head down, her dark hair curtaining her face.

'I'm tired.' There was bewilderment in her voice and he turned her round to face him.

'You're hurt,' he corrected softly. 'We're in a no-win situation. You're terribly afraid and you won't tell me why, and I'm making matters worse because...'

His voice stopped and she looked up then, her teeth biting into her lower lip, her little action drawing his gaze.

'Don't do that!' he ordered, restlessly impatient. 'It makes you look guilty and makes me feel worse than ever.' His finger moved to her lips, forcing them to part, moving to the tender moisture inside.

It was erotic, possessive, and the party came forcefully back to her mind, the sort of people there.

'What—what would they think...? We just walked out...' she said thoughtlessly.

'They'll think we're back here, of course.' His face darkened, and Emma's face flushed as she thought of the evening and the way she had wanted to stay in his arms. She might be innocent, but she had not lived on another planet. She knew where things had been leading and it was only now that it frightened her. It hadn't frightened her then. She suddenly looked a little wild and he moved restlessly, his hands cupping her face.

'I want you. You're not so innocent, so afraid that you don't know that,' he said thickly.

Fear was laced with all other feelings, and she went stiff, cold. Would he think it all right to begin again here, where there were no people likely to burst in on them? She was torn by feelings, knowing that if things went any further than they had done at the party she would start to panic and scream. Maybe Jake wouldn't want to stop this time?

'Please!' she gasped frantically, and his hands tightened on her face.

'Don't, Emma! Don't be like this with me,' he ordered harshly. 'Tell me why you're so afraid. How can I help if I don't know?'

'I—I can't tell you!'

She wouldn't look at him and he growled angrily.

'You *will*!' he rasped, lashing his arms around her. 'You've got to!'

She began to struggle and he let her go at once, his face tight and pale.

'Tell me who attacked you. You've been terrified of me since we first met and I've given you no cause to be. You *wanted* to be in my arms tonight at that party. You went up in flames, but now you're terrified again because you've had time to think about it. I want to know why. Who attacked you?'

'Nobody.' She closed her eyes tightly and stood stiffly in front of him.

'You've got to be lying. Don't I rate the truth? Nobody of your age nowadays is so sexually naïve, not to the extent that they don't know exactly what they're inviting when they look at a man as you keep looking at me. Anybody with any experience of men at all would have turned and run the moment they saw that cosy storeroom. You didn't. You looked at me with those helpless eyes and just did exactly as I wanted. It was what you wanted too, and yet you're terrified as soon as I give you the chance to think about it. Why?'

She felt safer when he was angry. Her mind acknowledged this with a surge of misery. She didn't even understand herself, although she should have. She just went on standing there, saying nothing, and for a second she thought he was going to explode with rage, but he evidently knew it was useless.

'All right,' he muttered. 'You can go to bed. Don't let me detain you. You can lock the door too,' he added in a hostile voice. 'I have no need to come in here and, my God, I wouldn't dare. No doubt you'd scream the place down. The whole street would be here, hammering at the door.'

What did the whole street think now? The thought suddenly occurred to her and she turned to look at him, her face still pale.

'What do they...?'

He had no trouble following her thoughts and he turned away furiously, jerking the door wide open.

'Oh, they think I'm right in this bedroom with you, running my fingers through that long dark hair, caressing that delicate little body, kissing those innocent soft lips! They *know* what I'm doing. It's what I always do—perfectly normal!'

He went out, slamming the door, and Emma bit into her lip to stifle the cry of denial and jealousy that came surging into her throat. She almost ran to the door, locking it as he had suggested, not because she thought he would come—he wouldn't do that, his contempt had been real enough. She locked it so that he wouldn't be able to come if he heard the weeping that was even then beginning.

It had never before occurred to her that she could be jealous of anyone who came close to Jake, that she could feel as bereft to see him holding another woman as she had done at the party, that she should feel such anger as when he had carelessly slapped that girl with the artist across the street.

She had met him in strange circumstances, and his life before that had never even crossed her mind. She knew of his fame, his wealth, but she had somehow never thought of him in other circumstances. It was almost frightening the way she had grown close to him. He almost seemed to be hers.

CHAPTER SEVEN

THE next day Jake was once again the dark and silent stranger who had met Emma on the moor and frightened her. The drive back to Devon was long and silent, her night of misery keeping her quiet, Jake's angry indifference deepening the misery until she wanted to stop the car and get out, to just walk away.

'I've told the garage to collect your car and repair it,' he suddenly said tightly. 'As you won't accept a fee for posing for me, I thought it was a good idea to take on the repair of your car.'

'I can pay for it.' She was instantly defensive, quite sure he was making certain she could leave as soon as the portrait was finished.

'No doubt,' he muttered acidly. 'However, *I'm* paying for it. It will ease my conscience, especially after last night.'

It was an effective way of silencing her, at least, and she sat quite still for the rest of the journey, her face unhappy, not that Jake looked at it.

Misery changed to shock and embarrassment when she saw a very expensive-looking car parked at the front of Credlestone Hall. She knew that car. She had been in it plenty of times. Somehow Gareth had found her, and she was filled with panic. What would Jake say? What would he think?

Whatever he thought, he said nothing, and his dark face gave nothing away either. He simply drove around to the back of the house and parked. Her car wasn't there. The garage had obviously collected it and Emma felt trapped.

Now was the time to stop Jake and explain about Gareth but she hadn't the nerve. He was so silent that she might just as well have never known him. There was nothing for it but to walk into the house and face things.

'You've got a visitor, Miss Shaw.' Mrs Teal popped out of the kitchen and beamed at her. 'Luckily he's only just arrived. I was just telling him you were in London when I saw the car coming back. I've put him in the sitting-room,' she confided as she went back to her work.

Emma took a deep breath and went to the door, her teeth biting at her lip. It was going to be very embarrassing. If Gareth raised his voice Jake would hear him, even in the studio. She opened the door and faced what had to be faced.

It was bewildering to see Gareth, as if she hadn't seen him for years and didn't know him. Surely he had put on a lot of weight? He seemed thick-set, almost middle-aged, and she had never noticed so much grey in his hair before. She realised she was merely comparing him with Jake's lean darkness, and Gareth took her heightened colour to be a sign of welcome.

'Emma! Darling! I've found you.' He stood and made a move towards her but as quickly stopped, and Emma didn't need second sight to know that Jake had not gone to the studio; he had walked in right behind her.

The sight of him seemed to baffle Gareth, and he looked suspiciously at her.

'I went to the flat,' he explained. 'Your friend Sue told me you'd come here. Well, she didn't know exactly where, but she remembered you'd said Credlestone Hall. She said you were staying with your uncle.' He shot an enquiring look at Jake, and Emma stumbled into speech.

'Er—yes, well, this is my uncle's house.'

'But he's in Africa at the moment,' Jake added coolly. 'Emma is staying with me.'

'I'm working here,' Emma got in quickly. She shot a reproachful glance at Jake that just earned her a sardonic look. 'Er—this is Gareth Forbes,' she said quickly. 'Jake Garrani,' she told Gareth.

'The artist? *That* Garrani?' Gareth seemed stunned and more suspicious than ever. So far he hadn't had time to be anything but shocked—events had overtaken him.

'*That* Garrani,' Jake agreed with a wry look at Emma. 'You seem to have read the same script.'

Gareth almost shook himself out of lethargy and moved towards Emma again.

'Darling, what do you mean—working? You know you're not fit to work, and who needs a physiotherapist out here?'

'Well, I do,' Jake interrupted drily. 'It's awfully bad for the back, standing at an easel all day. But, as a matter of fact, she'd not doing her normal work. She's working for me, and it's not hard. Usually she reclines on a couch.'

Gareth's face darkened and Emma rushed in quickly before Jake got her into further mischief.

'I'm posing for Mr Garrani,' she said firmly. 'Will you stay for lunch, Gareth?' She wasn't quite sure if she had the right to invite him, but she couldn't think of anything to say to smooth matters over, and at least he looked pleased.

'Of course. Finding my little runaway has been an exhausting business. Say you'll come back with me, Emma, and I'll really enjoy my lunch.'

'No doubt she'll be back when the portrait's finished,' Jake said bitingly. 'Not long now and then she's all yours. If you'll excuse me, I have to go out.' He just walked out of the room, and Gareth beamed all over his face, coming towards Emma to take her in his arms, and she backed off rapidly.

'We've been through all this,' she reminded him fiercely. It was utterly imperative that he didn't touch her because she suddenly saw him as he really was and she knew if he put his hands on her she would fight madly, and this time it would be in anger, not fear.

'I can't manage without you, Emma,' he said bitterly. 'I'm even prepared to get a divorce.'

'Not for me.' Emma stood stiffly by the door. 'I'm sorry you had this long journey but I made it quite clear I didn't want to see you again.'

His face darkened with anger and he looked at her scathingly.

'Found another meal-ticket, have you?' he grated crudely. 'I'm surprised Garrani fell for the childlike air. If ever there was a man of the world it's him. I didn't know you wanted experience, or I could have more than satisfied you; maybe not as much as Garrani, though. There haven't been many other women except my wife. Garrani takes his pick on two continents. I suppose you've discovered that. You don't look quite so bewildered as you used to.'

'I think you'd better go,' Emma said flatly, her face hot with shame.

'Maybe I should,' he sneered. 'He's probably hurrying back, ready for you to take up that reclining position.'

He just slammed out of the house, and Emma sat down abruptly. It would have been almost amusing if she could just get a hold of her trembling feelings. Her of all people! Gareth thought she was living with Jake, and it was quite clear what Jake thought.

She ate a lonely meal and then sat pretending to read. Jake didn't come in for lunch and he was still not there when Mrs Teal left. Facing Jake would be impossible

after this, and when her car came back she would have
to go. The portrait came to her mind and she felt a wave
of guilt. She couldn't let Jake down. Still, he might not
want to finish it now.

He came just as it was getting dark, and every nerve
tightened when she heard his car. She was sitting like a
mouse when he walked into the room, but she made
herself speak.

'I thought you might be staying out for dinner.'

'Maybe I would have done, but there was just the off
chance that you were here alone.'

'Why wouldn't I be here alone? You know Mrs Teal
leaves before dark.' Emma looked up at him miserably
and he simply avoided her eyes, his mouth twisting
derisively.

'It wasn't Mrs Teal I had in mind. There was always
the possibility that you'd invited Forbes to stay the night.'

'As if I would,' Emma gasped. 'In the first place, this
is not my house and, in the second place——'

'In the second place, it's not private enough with me
here,' he finished harshly.

'He's—he's just someone I knew.'

'Really?' He looked down at her coolly. '"Emma
darling"? You knew him well, I take it?'

'Yes. I knew him well, or at least I thought I did, but
we were not... If you think——'

'I don't think!' he grated. 'I don't need to think when
I see a man looking at you like that. Well, at least it's
solved one problem. I know why you were on the run.
What happened? Lovers' quarrel?'

'I don't have lovers!' Emma snapped, hurt enough to
be angry with him. 'Hasn't that dawned on you yet? I'm
odd. After all, you said it. You noticed it at once. My
relationship with Gareth is none of your affair.'

'No, it isn't,' he rasped, but apparently he couldn't
keep quiet. 'You're young enough to be his daughter!'

'Maybe that's why I thought I could manage. Maybe that's why I thought...' Emma turned away from the black anger and stood looking into the fire, dropping the subject completely. It hurt to argue with Jake, to hear his harsh condemnation, and he didn't know her at all really. It had hurt too to hear Gareth say that Jake knew a lot of women. Of course he did. What had she expected? 'How long will the portrait take?' she asked in a subdued voice. 'I'll go as soon as it's finished.'

'It's almost finished now,' Jake informed her tightly. 'At a pinch I could finish it from memory.'

'Then I'll go when my car comes back.'

'Please yourself. Far be it from me to spoil any plans you made with Forbes.'

'I didn't make any plans,' Emma murmured, almost in a whisper. 'I'm right back where I started.'

If he heard the misery in her voice he chose to ignore it; his own temper controlled him.

'Surely not,' he sneered. 'He came all this way to find you—his little runaway.'

'To no point whatever,' Emma disclosed bitterly. 'He's married.' She turned on him angrily, tired of his scornful attack. 'Now you know everything. Just leave me alone.'

For a moment he stood looking at her, and then he turned and walked out, his last remark thrown over his shoulder as usual.

'I don't know everything. I damned well don't know *anything*!'

She was back in the studio next day, back to her pose, and Jake was as silent as ever. He was wearing dark blue jeans, a white sweat-shirt that emphasised his broad shoulders, and her eyes did what they always did; followed him around.

Even when Mrs Teal had gone and the room began to get slightly dusky, he kept on working, and the air was almost electric, singing with Jake's moodiness and Emma's awareness. Since last night he had not spoken to her at all. She had put out the meal, and he had walked in and sat down to eat in silence. Emma had gone to bed, too hurt for tears, and now they choked her.

He glanced at the window and put his brush down at last.

'The light's gone, but it doesn't matter any more. It's finished,' he said quietly. 'From now on you're free.'

It had a very final ring, dismissive, cold, and Emma stared at him with an empty feeling growing inside her.

'Can I see it now?' She hardly dared ask, but it seemed only reasonable.

'No!' The slashing hostility of his voice made her jump, and she looked away quickly, her eyes filling with tears, her fingers fumbling to get the buttons of her dress fastened, doing it all wrong and having to start again.

'Why the desperate rush?' he jeered cruelly, walking over and looking down at her. 'You're almost completely decent. I don't expect you look any different from any other woman. When you've seen one you've seen them all. One breast is pretty much like another.'

The tears welled up but she fought them down, a sob rising in her throat that she couldn't contain, its small muffled unhappiness loud in the silence. Her hands trembled and she shook her head despairingly, her fingers no longer capable of fastening anything. He could hurt her so bitterly.

With a muffled oath, Jake crouched down beside her, his fingers taking over, moving to the buttons, and she dared not look at his face.

'Stop being so frantic,' he ordered roughly. 'You're just like any other woman, after all.'

His fingers stilled on the buttons and he gave a shaken sigh.

'Oh, hell, what am I saying?' he groaned. He leaned forward, clasping her waist, his face buried against her as his lips sought the warmth of her skin in the deep shadowed valley between her breasts. 'Emma! Let me touch you, let me hold you,' he begged huskily. 'I won't hurt you, I swear it.'

He wasn't capable of waiting for a reply. His lips came to hers, his hands moving to capture her face, holding her still as his mouth crushed her own.

'Don't cry. Don't cry, Emma,' he murmured against the wet smoothness of her cheeks. 'Am I hurting your leg?'

He suddenly stood and lifted her, holding her against him, walking with her out of the room and into the fire-lit warmth of the sitting-room. She was still crying quietly, the hurt at his words not at all gone, and he put her on the settee in front of the fire, gathering her to him, caressing her face.

'I didn't mean it,' he said thickly. 'You've got me mindless, irrational. I can't even begin to think straight any more. I want to hold you, touch you, look at you. I have to see you every day, and if I come near I know it's almost certain to drive you to hysteria. You don't even know what you're doing to me, do you?'

His dark eyes roamed over her face, a deep, moody look that moved to her white neck and the shadows of her breasts. He swallowed hard, his face tight, his eyes half closed.

'You're not like anyone else, Emma,' he assured her tautly. His lips came to her neck, lingering and warm, tasting her skin, and when she made no move of anxiety his hand slid inside her dress, capturing her breast, moving over it passionately. She jerked with pleasure and he stopped, certain that she would scream out, but when he looked up at her the tears were gone. They lingered on her cheeks, on her dark lashes, but her eyes were closed in wonder, her whole body soft.

Jake moved beside her, gathering her close, his mouth on hers, teasing her lips open, his hand moving back to mould and caress her breast until she murmured against his lips.

'I know you want me, Emma,' he whispered against her mouth. 'What do you think it's doing to me, painting you, looking up and seeing those blue eyes watching me? I sometimes get the mad feeling that you're waiting for me to walk across and take you.' He sighed. 'Lord knows what would happen if I did!'

Her hand touched his face timidly and he looked at her with an agonised impatience.

'Do you imagine you've found a superman,' he asked huskily, 'somebody to look at you and never come near?'

His head bent quickly, his mouth finding the tight nub of her breast and closing over it, his hand in her back arching her upwards until she felt utterly possessed. More buttons opened beneath his searching fingers. The dress slid from her shoulders and Jake's lips moved over hers, discovering her slender waist, his tongue against her skin, his breathing harsh and unsteady.

It was his obvious desperation that sent the first shock wave of fear through her, and she fought it with everything in her, her hands clinging to him as his mouth came back to her breast. She wanted him so much to stay like this but she could not fight a lifetime of conditioning.

He was big, strong, a man. Her eyes opened and saw his dark head against her white skin, saw the power of him, the drive in him to possess her, and nothing could keep the fright at bay then; other pictures made by her imagination raced into her mind, and Jake was no longer there.

She arched stiffly, her body losing its soft acquiescence, her fingers tugging at his hair, fighting. Her legs kicked out and he looked up quickly, seeing the glazed terror in her eyes.

'Emma! Emma!' He shook her, and then his hand cupped her face, forcing her eyes to look at him clearly. 'Emma, it's me. You're safe!'

The desperate pictures left her mind and she collapsed against him, sobbing bitterly, ashamed and filled with an aching need to be forever close to him, knowing it could never happen. Her tears were warm and wet against his face, and he held her tightly until only choking sobs sounded in the room.

Then he lifted her, fastening her dress, wiping her eyes and looking at her for a long time.

'Tell me,' he said simply. 'Tell me, Emma. This time you must.' He grasped her chin, his eyes fiercely determined when she looked up at him, and she just whispered her answer.

'It was my mother.' He let her go and she turned away, her face against the back of the settee, hiding, but when she started she couldn't seem to stop, and every last thing came out as she relived her long nightmare in the open for the first time.

'My father was the vicar at St Jude's when he died, but we weren't always there. Before that, when I was little, we had a big old vicarage in the country. I can still remember it. I can remember it even when I don't want to. There were gardens, big gardens with high yew hedges, and the vicarage and the church were a long way from the village. I was about seven then and my father had a huge parish. He had a little black car and he went all round the parish in that. He—he was quite a lot older than my mother—in his late forties—so there were no other children and I used to be alone a lot. I talked to myself.'

'So did I,' Jake interrupted softly. 'So do most children. Go on, Emma. Tell me what happened when you were a little girl.'

She turned away again, her voice very low.

'There was a cupboard under the stairs. I used to play there with all my imagined friends and my toys. If I left the door open a crack I had enough light. My father used to have services at another church too, alternate Sundays, and we used to go with him. I had German measles one time, though, and I couldn't go, so we stayed at home, my mother and I. I was playing under the stairs and she was having a bath.'

Tears began to run down her face and she wiped them frantically away, her voice choked as she went on.

'I heard a noise and I was scared. It was a long way up to the bathroom in that old house, so I kept very still and looked through the crack. There were two men. They were going from one room to another, taking our things, putting them into a bag. I thought they must be mad, but I suddenly knew that they thought the house was empty.'

Her voice broke and Jake pulled her to him, holding her close.

'Go on, Emma,' he said quietly.

'They went upstairs with the bag. I saw they had other bags too and I knew they'd come to get as much as they could. I should have shouted. I should have warned my mother, but I was too scared. I just hoped they wouldn't notice her, as they hadn't noticed me. They—they did, though. I—I heard them laughing, frightening laughter, and then nothing. She never screamed or shouted, and I know it was because she was trying to pretend she was alone in the house, praying that I'd keep quiet. After—after they'd gone I went upstairs and she was lying on the bedroom floor. She—she'd managed to pull a sheet over her and I didn't know what had happened. I only found out later from other people; the children at school heard and they talked about it.'

Jake was holding her so tight that it hurt, his hand pressing her head to his shoulder, but she had to finish now. It was the only time in her life that she had told anyone.

'We moved then, almost at once, but she never got over it. She was pale and quiet, and one day she went out and never came back. It was only when I was a teenager that my father told me she had been found and she was dead. He put locks on all the doors in the house, and took me to school and brought me back, even when I was at high school. I was supposed to be constantly on guard. He was terrified of something happening to me, so, you see, I never really had the chance to meet anyone until I started my training at the hospital, never on my own.'

Jake was rocking her steadily, and she cried even more.

'It was my fault, Jake. I should have screamed, run out, warned her.'

'Shh!' he soothed. 'Where was there to run for a little girl so far from the village? She was protecting you. It's what mothers do, and you were too scared to move. That's what little girls do.' He sighed against her hair. 'I suppose I can understand your father, but he simply drove it all the more deeply into your mind with his obsession with locks and safety. No wonder you behave as you do.'

He lifted her face, wiping the tears.

'You've got to let it go, Emma, the guilt and the fear. A little fear in this harsh world is only sensible, self-protective, but you're not even that. You walk out on to a foggy moor. You let me make love to you . . .'

'I—I'm not afraid of you,' she said quickly, choking on tears, and he shook his head in disbelief.

'Even if you're not, it's only natural to . . .'

Her bewildered and unhappy face seemed to be too much for him. He held her tightly for a minutes and then stood.

'I'll get you some tea and you can just eat a little of what Mrs Teal has left. Then you can go to bed. Things will be better in the morning.'

She was still shivering, though, when he urged her to bed, and he came quickly when she called out his name.

'What?' He stood in the doorway and looked at her patiently.

'Stay with me, Jake,' she whispered, not one bit anxious about that. 'I don't want to be alone.'

'All right.' He switched off the light and walked to the bed, lying on top of the clothes and putting his arm round her. She felt peaceful at once and her eyes closed after a few seconds.

'Jake, will you be comfortable there?' she asked sleepily.

'I'll make out. Stop worrying about my comfort. Leave that to me,' he advised softly, and she fell asleep almost at once.

In the morning he was gone and she had no idea how long he had stayed. Somehow she felt that telling him had partly exorcised her fear, had partly laid the ghost to rest, but it had also made her feel pretty raw. Even after a night's sleep, she felt the anguish of the tears, the ache of the guilt, the way she had drawn Jake into her own private misery.

He wasn't at breakfast, and Mrs Teal told her he had already had his before she had arrived this morning.

'He seems to be very busy in the studio. I heard him going back and forth to his car too.'

It frightened Emma more than anything else could have done. She almost choked at her breakfast and finally gave up any pretence of eating it. She was scared

to face Jake. He had been kind last night but she felt
she had imposed on him, her raw feelings making her
more shy than ever.

She had to find out what he was doing, though, and
she went to the studio and walked in anxiously.

'Hello.' He looked up as she came in and she could
see that he really was busy. He was cleaning brushes and
packing them. His easel was already collapsed and
folded, the legs lashed together with a leather strap.
'Sleep well?' he added politely.

'Yes.' She just stood there and he got on without any
further comment. 'You—you really meant it, then?
You've finished the picture?'

He just nodded and carried on, and she summoned
up all her courage.

'Can I see it now?'

'No.' His voice was not annoyed, simply firm, and he
just went on packing as she stood there, feeling utterly
in the way.

'Aren't you going to do any others?'

'No,' he said quietly, not bothering to look round.
'I'm packing up. I'm leaving tomorrow morning.'

It was like a physical blow, so much so that her hand
grasped the corner of the settee he had not yet got around
to moving back to its place. He wasn't even looking at
her. His mind was completely on what he was doing, as
if she had hardly existed to him at all in any case.

'You—you said you had the house for a whole year.'

'That's right. I've decided to go, though.'

It was almost impossible to speak clearly. The whole
of her world seemed to be shattering, drifting away from
her grasp, emptiness filling the gap.

'Shall you go to London, to your flat?'

'I'll have to call at my flat to get a few things, but I
don't leave much in England. There's little here that ap-
peals to me. I'm hardly ever here. I've got a few things

in New York and London, but mostly I live in Italy.
That's where I'm going. I'll probably fly out tomorrow
afternoon or the next day.'

Emma couldn't listen to any more. She just turned
and walked out while she still felt able to move. She was
too shocked even to cry, and she went upstairs to get her
coat and scarf and then let herself out of the house
without a word, making herself walk and walk, taking
all the morning and not coming in at lunchtime. Even
as she walked, she didn't think. Nothing could penetrate
the depth of icy misery that gripped her mind. She was
frozen up inside. Numb with grief as she had never ever
been before. Jake was leaving and he was leaving now.
She would never see him again.

Even when she returned, she could not eat her lunch.
She went into the sitting-room and crouched on the
settee, looking at the fire, staying there even when Mrs
Teal left, and Jake never came in. She could hear him
hammering at something and she heard him coming from
and going to his car. He was packing to leave. She tried
to read, but every word swam before her eyes with no
meaning at all, and when it got dark she went to the
kitchen and got the meal ready, thankful that it was
another casserole she couldn't spoil. She felt incapable
of doing anything.

Jake ate in silence, and when he came into the sitting-
room with his coffee she had got to the stage where she
wished he would not. It was impossible to keep the misery
from her face and impossible to speak.

It was Jake who spoke.

'Shall you stay here when I've gone?' he asked quietly
into the silence. 'If you're staying then some arrangement will have to be made for the nights. Perhaps
Mrs Teal and her husband would be prepared to move
in with you for a while? Would you like me to ask her?'

'I can ask her,' Emma whispered. He was so calmly matter-of-fact, planning to leave and determined to make sure she was left in some sort of safety. He was probably sorry for her now.

'Jake. Can I go with you?' she suddenly asked frantically, looking at him with wild hope.

The dark eyes held hers.

'I want you,' he reminded her quietly. 'If you come with me you'll be living with me, and I don't mean just in the same house. Any other arrangement is impossible. I know myself too well.'

He was still sitting in the chair opposite, watching her face, and her eyes left his, a frantic feeling inside her. Her hands clenched and unclenched and it was even difficult to breathe. She knew he watched this display of emotion and she would have liked to hide away, but there was nowhere to hide.

Days ago she had quietly admitted to herself that she loved Jake, that without him there would be a great empty space where her life should have been. He was offering her the chance to stay with him, to be with him, but she knew it was impossible. Faced with so much physical contact, she would freeze up, panic. Hadn't she done that last night for very little?

'I can't go. You know I can't, Jake.'

She turned her head away and he stood smoothly, no sign that her refusal had at all angered or disappointed him.

'All right. It was only the answer I expected.'

He moved to the door and she felt a wave of fright, the same terror that had swept through her when she had realised he was intent on leaving.

'Jake!'

He turned back and looked at her, his face quite cool.

'Don't let it worry you,' he advised quietly. 'It's no big deal, Emma. You're not the first girl, and I don't expect you'll be the last. Just make sure you don't stay in this house alone, that's all. Eric wouldn't like that one bit.'

He walked out, and she stood staring at the place where he had been a second before. She was not the first girl and she wouldn't be the last! It hurt like a dull knife-thrust, so much that she couldn't move. Jake would go and never give her another thought. He would live his life as he had always done. Her mind went spinning to the scene in London, the artists, the women there, the easy familiarity. Jake had been a different person there. He had not been the silent, dark man she had known in this house. He had laughed, danced, his eyes alight with interest as he had watched the women there, and they were used to it, they had come to him eagerly.

She had gone to him eagerly too, and she wouldn't be the last. He had said that. She walked slowly up to bed, not surprised to see that Jake's light was already out. He was getting an early night, ready for his journey to London and then to Italy, ready to walk out of her life forever.

Sleep only came when she was exhausted, and even then it was broken by dark, unhappy dreams. The dark dreams had always been there, a burden she had carried for years, but they faded to grey phantoms beside the new pictures of loneliness that filled her head.

CHAPTER EIGHT

EMMA was awake early and went silently down the stairs to make tea and sit at the table alone, waiting for her last glimpse of the tall dark stranger who had changed . her whole life. He was down before she even knew he was awake. He walked into the kitchen and looked startled to see her.

'An early bird?' he queried wryly. 'Is there any tea left?'

'I'll make some more. I don't think it will be too hot by now.'

His dark brows drew together in the old familiar scowl at this little clue that she had been here for some time, but he just nodded and walked out again, and she knew he would be packing his clothes. The studio had been cleared yesterday. Within a very short time he would be ready to leave and he would want to be off. He had a long way to go. Italy was so far away.

She made the tea but she couldn't call him. Just to say his name was more than she could bear. He was moving briskly about and she heard his car door slam as he put his cases in it. Soon he would be slamming the door and driving off. He would be driving out of her life forever.

She was so wound up inside that she even thought she heard the car start, and a wave of terror seemed to wash right over her, so badly that her skin suddenly chilled. She would never see Jake again and the thought was unbearable. She flew out of the room, making her leg work, the pain she was inflicting on herself ignored.

He was coming from the back door towards the stairs, and he stopped as he saw her rushing towards him. Emma stopped too, leaning against the banister, clinging to it for support, her breathing as unsteady as if she had run up a steep hill.

'I thought you'd gone!'

'I am going.' He looked at her steadily and she burst out with the thought uppermost in her mind.

'Take me with you, Jake! I want to be with you. Please don't leave me.'

Her face was pale, her eyes enormous, and he walked slowly forward until he was looking down at her. His eyes seemed to search her soul and his arm came round her, drawing her tightly to him.

'I want to take you with me, but if you come with me you'll sleep with me,' he reminded her slowly. 'I'm leaving here because I can't stay and simply look at you any longer. Do you really know what it means to come with me, to live with me?'

'Yes, I know,' she whispered shakily.

He looked down at her for a long time and then drew her closer still, every inch of him taut.

'Once we leave this house,' he murmured, 'your chance of changing your mind is gone. I'll simply take you with me anyway. I won't be able to let you go. You've got me as desperate as you sound,' he added roughly.

His lips closed over hers, strong, cool and possessive, kissing her until she was shaking in his arms, until he had to hold her close to steady her and she wasn't left in any doubt that he wanted her.

'Go and pack your things,' he said thickly, his lips against her hair. 'I'm ready to leave. I'll make some breakfast and we'll be off as soon as Mrs Teal arrives.'

'What are you going to tell her?' Emma whispered, the reality of the situation very clear.

He drew his head back and looked down at her.

'Do you care enough to come with me in spite of your fears?'

'Yes.' If he left her she couldn't face anything. That dark restless face would haunt her days and nights for the rest of her life. Nothing seemed to have a purpose any more without Jake.

'Then leave her to me,' he said softly. 'Get your packing done.'

The feeling of breathless unreality was still there as she sat beside Jake on the flight. She seemed to have stepped from one life to another. In her uncle's house there had still been around her something of her past, and even Jake had been tied to some extent by the surroundings and the restrictions of life in the house on Dartmoor.

Now he was not the same. He seemed to have changed from the moment they had boarded the plane. It was an Italian plane and the flight crew knew him, breaking into warm smiles and greeting him in Italian. As soon as he spoke to them Emma knew that the man she had thought she knew was only a mere facet of Jake Garrani. She watched him now surreptitiously as he sat beside her, ironic, slightly disdainful, utterly confident. She had placed her life into his hands and she realised how little she knew him.

'Comfortable?' Those dark eyes turned on her and she nodded, looking away out of the window. He turned her back, his warm palm against her face. 'Frightened?'

'A bit. I—I've never flown before.'

A faint smile played around his lips and his hand slid to her neck, his fingers moving beneath the collar of her silk shirt, finding the warmth of her nape, pulling her forward.

'That wasn't the fright I was speaking about, and you know it,' he said quietly. He urged her forward until she was looking up into his eyes. He seemed to be so much bigger than she was, so supremely certain of his own power. The irony was there for her to see, mocking her, none of the patient man left, but a flare of excitement raced through her even so, his fingers on her nape sending waves of forbidden delight through her.

He watched her reaction to him and his smile grew before he bent his head and covered her mouth with his own, his lips open, lingering, moving insistently, claiming hers with an arrogant possession, as if they were already lovers.

A polite cough interrupted them and Emma met the amused eyes of the stewardess.

'Drinks, Signor Garrani?' She looked at him admiringly and he smiled, his eyes flashing over her dark, vivacious face in male admiration.

'*Grazie*.' He helped himself from the trolley and handed Emma a drink. It was a brandy and she would normally have shuddered, but she drank it with a sort of determined desperation, trying to let the warm liquid drown the wave of jealousy that had swept over her. She would never have Jake to herself, not really. Even if she managed...

He slid his arm around her, moving her drink to the table, urging her close, whispering to her in Italian.

'What does that mean?' The moment he touched her her doubts tried to fly away.

'It means you're as transparent as a child, as easy to read as a book.' He lifted her face, his lips over hers. 'In Florence I'll teach you to live.'

It was the first time he had mentioned where they were going. She had simply followed him without question.

'We're going to Florence?'

He nodded, his eyes moving over her lips like a caress.

'I live there. I work there. It's really my home. There's no other place that I owe any allegiance to.' His lips brushed hers lightly, and then he leaned back, keeping

her close. 'The flight's not too long, and then you can
see where you'll be living.'

'If—if I don't like it...?' she murmured, glancing up
at him.

'If you don't like it I'll take you to New York.' He
looked down at her, his dark eyes intent. 'Anywhere,'
he said. 'The only thing you can't have is escape. You
begged to come with me. You're here. I'm keeping you.'

It gave her a funny feeling, trapped, permanent, but
belonging. She relaxed against his strong shoulder and,
after a night of turmoil, she slept.

Crowds were everywhere. So many people that it was
alarming. As they had landed Emma's anxiety had re-
surfaced, this time with an added fear that she would
somehow be separated from Jake and never be seen
again. There was nothing anxious about Jake. He had
two porters in tow at once and they marched to a car
that was already waiting, a smiling Italian at the wheel.
He sprang out and came to greet them, fussing over the
luggage, tipping the porters and then sliding into the
driving-seat as Jake sat Emma in the back and moved
in beside her for the drive to Florence.

She seemed to be forgotten instantly as Jake leaned
over the passenger-seat and talked non-stop to the driver
in Italian and now, as they entered the city, they both
seemed to be ignoring the traffic, and after a few seconds Emma couldn't bear to look. She closed her eyes
and left things to chance.

'Emma? Are you all right?'

Jake noticed her and was back beside her at once, but
she smiled and opened her eyes, carefully avoiding
glancing at the road.

'No. Just don't tell me when we're going to crash. I'd
rather not know.'

He laughed and took her hand.

'It's no worse than London.'

'You've got to be joking!' Emma gasped. 'Anyway, in London there are rules, and by and large drivers follow them.'

Jake translated this to the driver, who seemed to have got most of it anyway. He was grinning widely.

'You will arrive safely, *signorina*,' he promised. He seemed to be going on two wheels and Emma reserved judgement, but she followed Jake's direction and gazed out of the window at the beauty of Florence by night.

Before long the crowds thinned and they drove down wide avenues edged with trees, the car crossing a bridge that spanned a wide river, which Jake told her was the Arno, and then they were turning into a secret, narrow street, the car slowing, and she knew with a flutter of her heart that they had arrived.

The house was a surprise. The car drove along past towering walls, secret and impregnable, and then as Jake got out to open a high solid gate they drove into a courtyard, and she discovered that the walls that fronted the road were the back walls of the house. The secrecy was complete, and the house was high, oddly beautiful, the courtyard lit by old lamps that hung from the walls.

'You live here?'

Jake helped her out and she stood gazing around, her eyes going from the wrought iron of the balconies to the long gleaming windows.

'*Sì, signorina*,' Jake mocked, and he smiled wryly. 'You expected a slum?'

'I didn't know what to expect. Is your studio here?'

'Yes. It's large, well equipped and it's right at the top of the house—private.'

It brought her back to the height. There would be plenty of steps here. There had been something mocking in Jake's voice, as if he was goading her, informing her

that she certainly would never make it up to that studio.
It brought unease, but she was not left uneasy for long.

They seemed to be being attacked by a small, excited
woman dressed in black, and Jake turned from Emma
to hug the woman to him, kissing her on both cheeks.
She was old, her brown cheeks wrinkled, but her eyes
were black and lively.

'This is Antonia,' Jake told Emma. 'She looks after
me. She looked after my mother and father too.' He
glanced down at the inquisitive little face and nodded
towards Emma. 'Signorina Shaw,' he explained.

'*Bella!*' She looked mischievously at Jake and spoke
very quickly, something that amused Jake, but he refused to translate and before Emma could get embarrassed she was taken into the house, walking under
glittering lights into a hall that seemed to have a marble
floor. The stairs swept down, the banisters gilded, and
again there was the cool glow of marble.

'Is this all marble?' She couldn't believe it was real.

'It is,' Jake assured her. 'This is an old house. It
probably dates from the sixteenth century. I've lived here
for most of my life. When houses like this were built it
was normal to use marble. The stairs are marble to the
next floor, and then wooden and quite ordinary.'

'They're a long way up,' Emma murmured, feeling
tired and too excited to be anything like normal herself.
It brought a low, dark laugh from Jake and he walked
to the side of the hall, pressing a switch. There was a
smooth sound of machinery, and to Emma's astonishment a lift descended from above. It was gilt, a thing
of beauty itself but quite extraordinary, its progress slow
and somehow very dignified as it moved into sight close
to the wall. She just stared.

'My grandmother lived here with us,' Jake explained.
'I just remember her. She was a very old lady and
couldn't face the stairs. My father was a highly inventive

man. He planned this and had it made. It suits the
Florentine mind to delve into the impossible. An ordinary lift was out of the question, too ugly. My father
despised the ugly.'

'It's like a golden bird cage!' Emma exclaimed, and
Jake laughed softly.

'Full marks. That's just what was planned. My grandmother was like a small black bird, like Antonia. I still
remember her riding up in this and gazing down at me
with reprimanding eyes. Let's see you do it.'

He had her into the lift before she could be scared,
and he simply stepped out and watched as she stood quite
petrified in the golden cage that lifted her smoothly upwards. She grasped the bars and the whole thing began
to amuse her; her face lit up with delighted laughter, and
Jake stood below, watching her slow ascent, his eyes on
her glowing face, his gaze narrowed and intent.

She was out of his sight before she could blush at his
possessive look, and when the strange lift came to a stop
he was almost there, his footsteps quick and strong on
the marble steps.

'There! What about that?' His eyes were laughing into
hers and she stepped out on to a long landing that seemed
to run the width of the house, her eyes bright with
pleasure as she looked around.

'Oh, Jake, it's so beautiful.' She turned and looked
at him, her face puzzled. 'I thought you said you used
to be poor?'

'True,' he agreed with a laugh. 'As a church mouse.'

'But this house...'

'Ah! I never said my family was poor. My father was
a goldsmith, a master. I had a life of ease all mapped
out for me, but I wanted to paint and he recognised my
talent. I trained here, and then I wanted to go to London.
He took my cheque-book away, got me a ticket, gave

me a reasonable amount of cash and told me to go and suffer.'

'How old were you then?' She was standing, looking up into his face, fascinated.

'Younger than you by a long way. My mother wept and begged, but my father was right. When you live close to the edge of things you develop an eye for people. You see more than the outward signs. Each face tells a deep story, and without that insight you're no good as an artist.'

She wondered what he saw in her face. Did he see her feelings clearly, or was he simply taking care of her? Perhaps it was just because he wanted her. She still could not believe that really. She was so ordinary and Jake was important, well known, a giant in his sphere. She was watching him with a kind of awe, and he smiled down at her.

'That expression may be good for my ego,' he murmured, 'but it doesn't do a lot for my self-control.'

She didn't know whether he was pleased or not. He simply took her arm and led her almost at once into a bedroom with huge double doors. It was quite breathtaking, the long windows open to the courtyard below, gauzy curtains drifting in the breeze. Everything was white, simple and clean, but it was a rich room, the pictures glowing, the few ornaments exquisite.

Her heart began to pound as the reality of being here returned with a rush, his words ringing in her mind. Was it to be here? Now? She walked across to look down at the courtyard and then turned, avoiding Jake's eyes.

'Did you paint the pictures?'

'Only one. The rest were done by friends. There's an artist, potter or goldsmith in almost every man in Florence.'

He knew she was scared but he never mentioned it, and she hid her trembling hands behind her.

'Do I sleep here?'

'Yes. Enrico will bring your cases up here in a minute.' He watched her intently. 'This is my room. I've slept here since I was a boy, improved it since I grew up. You sleep here.'

She felt her breathing slow to an almost painful pace, her heart fluttering. Could she cope? Would she fly into hysteria and anger him? Her eyes sought his, a desperate anxiety in them, and he looked at her steadily.

'Come here, Emma,' he commanded softly.

She had to obey, and he watched her walk towards him, his eyes sweeping over her, his arms reaching for her when she stood close.

'Look at me.' He locked her to him, his arms tight round her waist, and she raised blue eyes to his dark gaze. 'Silly girl,' he murmured softly. 'Have I ever behaved like a savage? When have you not been safe? Do you think I want you screaming in my arms? When this city, this new life has driven all the past away then you'll sleep here with me. Whenever you look at me with fear, whenever you tremble at the thought of a night in my arms, there'll be nobody in this room but you, Emma.'

She wanted him to stay and hold her, to let her enjoy the pleasure of his arms now that she felt safe again, to show her that he understood, but he did nothing of the sort. He simply let her go and walked out, and she heard him going quickly down the stairs as all the joy faded from her face. Nothing was wonderful when Jake walked away.

For a few days Jake did absolutely nothing but treat her like a visitor. He was pleasant, attentive and thoughtful. He showed her round the city during the day, took her out at night to dine, and seemed to be quite set on giving her a good time. He was not, however, at all close in any way. He seemed to treat Antonia and Enrico with

more warmth, and she began to feel nothing but captured, the amusing lift like a cage of gold that had been
waiting for her, Jake's polite conversation unreal. She
would have preferred his anger or scorn to his pleasant
indifference.

Even his brief flare of passion on the plane, his gentle
concern for her when she had first arrived, had gone.
Sometimes he simply disappeared for hours, and then
she sat in the courtyard or stayed in her room, lost and
terribly lonely, but too committed to Jake to think of
asking to leave and return to London.

She could have left. She could simply have walked
out. She had withdrawn all her savings before she had
left London, and she supposed, thinking about it, that
this was a reflection of the deep distrust she had of men,
even Jake. He wouldn't even be greatly concerned if she
did leave, she was sure of that. Any desire he had felt
for her seemed to have gone. Did he find her different
here? He was different in his own surroundings, the pull
of the fog-bound house on the moors gone. Maybe she
looked different to him too?

They were not too far from the river, and she slipped
out quietly one afternoon and walked slowly to it,
standing on the nearest bridge and watching the whole
gleaming length of it, the many bridges like lacy arches
across the broad water.

Enrico had been telling her about the Ponte Vecchio,
about the shops of the jewellers and goldsmiths that
made it famous, and she made her way there, jostled by
the crowds but determined to go, her mind pushing away
the realisation that Jake no longer even wanted her.

It was an astounding place, so many riches in such a
small area. Tourists crammed the whole length of it,
staring at the dazzling display of brilliant craftsmanship,
and Emma lingered for a long time, unable to take her
eyes from the beautiful jewellery, the lovely worked gold.

It was getting dark before she could bring herself to move, to make her way back to the house, and she discovered then just how far she had walked. By the time she came to the street where the houses secretly turned their backs to the road it was quite dark.

The gates were wide open, every light in the house blazing, and as she came across the courtyard Jake came striding from the house, his hand on the car door before he saw her. She had never seen him so angry, and neither apparently had Antonia and Enrico. They looked at her with relief, glanced at Jake's thunderous face and then discreetly disappeared.

He came over to her and said nothing at all, his dark eyes burning with rage, his lips in one tight line of temper, and then he took her arm, marching her to the door, swinging her up into his arms and striding along in silence when it became apparent that she could not run at his side.

He ignored the fancy little lift. His rage enabled him to take the stairs at some speed, two steps at a time, and Emma found herself inside the bedroom, the door slammed closed and Jake towering over her before she had really recovered from the shock of meeting him at all.

'Where have you been?' His voice was low and threatening, his face looking darker than it had ever done.

'I went out to look around, then I went to the Ponte Vecchio to see the jewellery. I—I didn't mean to be so late.'

'This is a major city, crowded with tourists, pockets of crime all over,' he informed her in a voice that was little more than a deep, frightening whisper. 'There are thieves, kidnappers, rapists...'

'Jake, you're frightening me!' Her hand came to his arm and he took it in his strong fingers, crushing it, hurting her.

'I mean to frighten you! Since I first saw you you've wandered about with no thought for your own safety. If I come near you you collapse, but you feel it perfectly normal to roam streets you've never seen before, to rub shoulders with strangers and come back after dark. In future you don't leave this house without me. In future you stay within sight of Enrico or myself!'

She stared at him in disbelief. He had been practically ignoring her for days, and now she was to be imprisoned.

'I *won't*! You can't keep me here like a prisoner!'

His hand released hers and he snatched her forward, his fingers biting into her shoulders.

'Leave, then. Go back to England. Ask me to put you on a plane!'

She was going to, her eyes angry too as she stared into his, but even in a rage she could not envisage the day without a sight of him; even the hard pressure of his fingers now was better than no contact with him at all. She looked down, her eyes filling with tears, and he jerked her head up, his dark, angry eyes searching her face.

'Well? Do you go back?'

She pressed her trembling lips together and closed her eyes, shaking her head slowly, the tears escaping to her cheeks.

'It's as well you don't want to,' he grated, 'because there's no way that I'll let you. You'll stay with me, and one day you'll sleep with me; until then you'll be kept safe.'

He suddenly pulled her closer.

'I thought you wouldn't be able to get back.' His arms came around her, crushing her. 'I thought somebody...'

She looked up at the harsh, harrassed sound of his voice, and his lips drove down on hers, heavily and almost cruelly. He was possessive, implacable, dominating her, his body restless against her, and it was minutes before he let her go at all. She almost fell, leaning against the wall as he turned to leave.

'If—if I really wanted to go...' she began shakily.

He turned back, the dark eyes pinning her fast.

'You made your decision when you asked me to bring you here,' he said quietly. 'On the plane I told you I'd take you anywhere. The only thing you can't have is escape, and I mean that. You're with me, and you're with me for as long as I want you!'

She half expected to hear the door locked on her, but it wasn't. For a long time she stood looking out of the window, her view confined to the lighted courtyard, Jake's words ringing in her mind, her own thoughts a turmoil of anxiety and bewilderment. He had been almost mindless with worry, his actions on the edge of violence. He never came near her, but he would not let her go. She had walked willingly into this and she had no sort of ability to walk out of it, with or without Jake's permission.

It seemed, however, to have brought a change of attitude in Jake. Instead of leaving the house so regularly he began to work, and the first that Emma knew of it was when she heard a young female voice and came out of the downstairs sitting-room to see Antonia letting a very vibrant-looking young woman into the house.

There was a lot of discussion, and Emma stepped back, unable though to bring herself to go far from the door. Jake came down from his studio in jeans and sweat-shirt, his thumbs hooked into the belt that surrounded his lean waist, and he stood and watched the girl in silence.

She was not at all nervous. She was quite sure of her own attraction, and Emma had to admit that she was very attractive indeed. Her black hair was a little wild, very curly and very long, a glossy mane to frame a vivid face. Red lips pouted at Jake and she went into a very

natural pose, turning slowly for his inspection. Emma
didn't need to be told that this was a model, and Jake's
eyes were narrowed in speculative interest, a smile playing
around his lips.

Her mind went back to her own days as Jake's model,
the silence of the studio, the way his eyes sometimes met
hers, the way he had kissed her to get the feeling into
her face that he was looking for. The old jealousy came
back, tearing into her as Jake stood talking in Italian to
the beautiful newcomer, his eyes moving over her constantly with mounting appreciation.

He said something in a low voice and nodded towards
the stairs, and the girl moved, walking away seductively,
Jake's eyes sensuous as they followed her movements.
He suddenly swung round, catching Emma watching,
and one dark eyebrow raised ironically. All her feelings
must have been there for him to see, and she turned and
walked quickly away, further into the room and out of
his sight, her mind only too aware that she limped still,
such a different movement from the swinging voluptuous walk the Italian girl possessed.

He came in, standing at the door, watching her, and
she ignored him, not trusting herself to speak. The same
jealous rage was inside her, the same need to shake him,
scream at him.

'Well, as an ex-model, what do you think of her?'

His taunting voice cut across the room and she swung
round to glare at him.

'Beautiful, sexy and cheap!'

'Oh, she doesn't come cheap. Her rates are higher than
most.' His voice was quietly jeering, and it drove away
any caution.

'I imagine they charge more to work nude.'

'It depends,' he mocked, a smile quirking his lips.

She didn't need the picture that this remark drew in
her mind. Her mind was already full to overflowing with

those. She came across furiously, ignoring the way his eyes roamed over her, ignoring the fact that she couldn't walk with that swaying ease that had drawn his attention to the girl now upstairs.

'I want to go home!'

Fury overrode any other emotion at that moment, and she did something she had never done with Jake or anyone else; she walked right up to him aggressively.

'No escape,' he murmured derisively, his height and the sheer animal power of him stopping her forward movement.

'You can't frighten me, Jake,' she raged. 'I'm tired of this game. I can't think why I'm here at all. I hate this house, this city, this country. I don't know you and I hate you anyway. I want to go home!'

He laughed down at her, catching her hand when she lashed out at him, pulling her forward and then lifting her against him until she was pressed close to his hard body.

'Jealous?' he taunted against her face, holding her fast as she struggled. He slid her to the floor and looked down at her, his hands moving down her back against her stiff and angry stance, deliberate seduction in his actions.

'Jealous?' he asked again. Before she could reply his mouth opened over hers, his fingers twisting in her hair, his hand across her hips, holding her against him. 'Come to me and I'll send her away. You know I wait for you every day. It's you I want.'

His words were murmured against her mouth but she tore her lips away, angry, frustrated and excited all at the same time, and he let her go, leaving her as if he had felt nothing at all.

'What am I expected to do in the meantime?' he queried drily, turning to the door.

It hit her like a shock, the pain of it making her clutch at her stomach, but he never even turned. When he had gone she walked to the courtyard and went to the gate, determined to walk away. The huge gates were locked.

If he had meant to torture he had certainly succeeded. Over the next few days the girl managed to arrive when Emma was downstairs and unable to avoid seeing her. The painting sessions went on for hours, lunch being taken up to both of them, and when Emma was upstairs she could hear the swift flow of Italian as Jake and the girl talked, none of the silence about him that she had always had to bear. There was laughter too, soft, low laughter that tore into her. There seemed to be nowhere to escape it, and every day the girl seemed to be more and more familiar with Jake, her eyes more and more admiring.

After two weeks she could bear it no longer. She went down early and collected her breakfast even before Jake was down. At least she didn't have to see the girl arrive. She closed the door, but the meal almost choked her, only the scalding hot coffee going down with any ease.

She left the rest and went to shower again, the sound of the water her chance of drowning out the sound of the arrival of the girl who was constantly with Jake. But she heard him on the stairs even as she came out in her robe, and she turned to the window, her hands pressed to her ears, unable any longer to bear that soft, seductive Italian murmured so freely between them.

CHAPTER NINE

EMMA was utterly unaware that Jake had come in; her
hands were pressed too closely to her ears. All she could
hear was the sound of her own tears, and as he wrapped
his arms around her and pulled her back against him
she jerked with surprise, her gasp lost into her own throat
as he spun her round and closed his lips over hers.

He had never shown tenderness before. Tenderness had
never seemed to be in him. Even when he had so obviously been worried about her there had been a deep-
seated anger there and the lingering feeling of his
harshness, but he was tender now. His hands caressed
her, his moving convulsively over hers.

'Emma, Emma. Sweet little fool,' he murmured over
her lips.

'Go! Go and get on!' she sobbed. 'Do what you do
every day!'

His fingers wiped her tears, his lips warm against her
cheeks.

'She's not here,' he murmured. 'She's not coming.'

'Then go and use your imagination,' she wept.

'My imagination is killing me!'

He swept her up into his arms, walking out of the
room before she could even think of struggling, and
striding up more stairs to the top of the house. She
couldn't bear to think that he was going to show her the
picture, and she struggled then, beating at him with her
fists.

'Don't, Jake. Don't do this to me. I don't want to see
the picture. I want to go home. I don't want to...!'

He put her down and forced her forward, his handling of her almost rough, making her face the easel, holding her shoulders when she tried to turn away, and it was unavoidable. The picture was there to see, finished with his whirlwind speed, the girl transformed, a laughing Italian peasant with no seduction in sight, the rolling countryside of Tuscany behind her, a beautiful, joyous thing.

'She—she's dressed!' It was the only thing Emma could think of saying.

'And well paid for her efforts,' Jake said thickly. 'Did you think I was making love to her? Did you imagine I could be up here with someone else when you were down there? Do you imagine anyone else ever comes into my mind? The picture is for you. It will hang in your room where you can see it. Maybe it will teach you a little trust!'

He sounded angry, and the fight went out of her as she turned to him, moving against him, her face in his shoulder, her teeth biting into her lip, ashamed of her wild jealousy.

'Jake...'

'Don't tell me you're sorry,' he muttered. He lifted her away and walked over to a small velvet settee, turning to look at her steadily. 'Come here, Emma,' he ordered quietly. 'Show me how sorry you are. Show me how you trust me.'

'I don't know how.' She looked up at him and his dark eyes held hers.

'You do. Stay here and let me paint you. Let me paint you as I've wanted to paint you since you came into my life out of the fog. Take the robe off.'

She looked away abruptly.

'I don't know if I can.'

'Well, that's a step forward,' he said softly. 'Normally you just say you can't. If you have doubts about it then it's all been worthwhile.' He held his hand out. 'Try it.'

She moved forward stiffly and he waited until she was sitting, his dark eyes holding hers. She could make no move to help, but his hands began to untie his belt that held the robe around her, their swift and certain movements mesmerising her.

'Jake!' There was the panic back in her voice as he slid the robe from her shoulders, and he bent his head, his lips covering hers as his hands drew the robe further away, the pressure of his mouth forcing her head back. Then he turned away without looking at her, leaving the robe half on, half off.

'Just pose as you did before,' he said in a perfectly normal, cool voice. 'Try to get into the exact pose you had, and don't think about me at all. You know I never see you when I'm painting. I only see the picture, and it's already in my mind.'

She moved slowly, her eyes fearfully on him, but he was busy, setting up a canvas, sorting his things out, and gradually her tense muscles eased, the panic drained away, and when he turned she was in a sort of trance, her eyes wide and blue, meeting his.

'That's perfect,' he said quietly. 'Who needs another model?'

He began to work, and after a minute every other worry faded. She was just as she had been before to Jake, a vase of flowers, a teapot, nothing at all but line, form and colour. Her tight breathing fell to a slow easy movement, her clenched fingers unwound and lay passively against the folds of the robe, and gradually a slight smile edged her lips as his eyes looked at her impersonally, his clever hands moving swiftly. If she put her tongue out he probably wouldn't even notice. The smile grew at the thought and his eyes flashed to hers, a moody, restless smile edging his own lips.

'You're beautiful.' His eyes moved back to his work. 'Just stay as you are.'

It wasn't difficult. He seemed not to see her at all, every movement as dispassionate as he had always been, and once again she was watching Jake, back where she had started, seeing the careless grace of him, the dark concentration of his eyes, the restless expressions that crossed his face. Every action made her more aware of him, her wide gaze following his movements.

He turned for more paint and looked up, his eyes meeting hers, and his face darkened as soft colour flooded her cheeks. For a second his eyes held hers, a naked desire in the dark gaze, and then he looked abruptly away, his hands moving again with that graceful speed.

She forgot that she sat still, half reclining on the dark blue velvet. It was another world, where she had never dared to tread. Their eyes met from time to time, the air singing between them, and after a long while he put down his brush and turned away.

'That's enough for now. I don't want you getting stiff.'

It reminded her that she wasn't anyone but herself, Emma Shaw, and the awakening clouded her face.

'I'm all right,' she muttered, her face downcast. 'My leg is nearly better.' It was a desperate little gesture and he recognised it. He swore under his breath, turning away until she had fastened the robe and got to her feet.

'I've had enough anyway,' he said brusquely. 'If you get dressed I'll take you out.'

She dressed later with a great feeling of bewilderment inside her, not really understanding until she remembered his face, the raw look in his eyes. He was making sure she trusted him, and a feeling of tenderness came into her too, lighting her face as she saw him waiting downstairs, brightening the whole afternoon.

They drove right out of Florence, up into the hills, to where a small village clustered around a ruined castle, silver-green olive groves brightening the brown earth. A farm stood isolated in fields and woodland, cypresses tall and dark behind it like the strong vertical strokes from an artist's brush against the golden sky. It was derelict, empty for years, and Jake smiled at her look of surprise as he drove up to it and invited her to get out.

'The last time I was here I bought this,' he informed her, his eyes running over it with an assessing look. 'It will make a very fine house.'

He began to show her what was planned, helping her over the rough stones, crouching with a stick to sketch plans into the soft earth. It was sunny and bright, and as she stood up again and looked across the countryside the sun touched the distant city, lighting up the roof of the cathedral and the Giotto bell tower, edging them with gold.

'Oh, look!' She pointed across, and Jake followed her gaze.

'Whenever the sun shines in Florence it shines on a glorious treasure,' he said quietly. 'I can't remember who said that, but it's true.' He looked at her. 'Do you feel trapped in the house?'

'Not any more.' She smiled and his eyes held hers, not smiling but with that look of dark vibrancy that could hold her spellbound. For a moment his eyes moved to run hungrily over the slender picture she made standing there. It made her feel warm and vulnerable, but he turned away suddenly.

'Let's go,' he said roughly. 'It's going to be months before this place is even half ready anyway.'

She was silent on the return journey. What had he meant? Would she still be here then? Had he been thinking that by then he would have lost all patience with her? The thought kept her silent for the rest of the evening, and to her dismay Jake was back to normal, the dark scowl on his face, the black eyebrows drawn together.

She thought he would have decided to let the whole matter of the pose drop by next morning, but after breakfast he stood and threw down his napkin with that edge of impatience that marked so many of his movements.

'Collect your robe and come up to the studio,' he said abruptly, walking out before she had time to get embarrassed.

She lingered about but he didn't come for her, and at last she made her way up the last flight of steps, her robe over her arm. She had been too nervous to undress down in her room, and Jake glanced at her without surprise. Apparently he knew how awkward she could be; at least, he looked as if he was thinking such thoughts.

'You can change behind the screen.'

She found that her hands had become icily cold. If he had continued yesterday she could have sat for hours and been totally unembarrassed, but this was a new beginning, without the tender caresses that had marked yesterday's start. When she came out she couldn't meet his eyes, and the robe was tightly around her.

'Just like yesterday.'

He was ignoring her and she did her best. It was impossible, though, to take up a languorous pose while her nerves were screaming, and Jake glanced up.

'It's not right. I'll have to move you.'

It had been bad enough on the one or two occasions when he had unfastened the buttons of her grey-blue dress for the other pose; now it was impossible to describe. She looked away and felt his hand on her leg, bending it slightly, his fingers flicking at her hair, easing her head away from its stiff angle, softening her shoulder.

'That's it.' He was breathing thickly but his hands were quite businesslike, and as he went back to his easel she dared to look up.

'Keep still!' he ordered roughly. 'We'll keep this session short.'

'I wish you could finish all in one go,' Emma said a little desperately. His eyes met hers. His movements stopped for a second.

'It would take all day and night. You wouldn't last out that long,' he assured her. He looked away abruptly. 'Neither would I,' he added harshly.

Gradually she relaxed again, watching him. She didn't care after a while if he realised it. Surges of feeling seemed to come and go with every movement he made, her lips parted, awareness of him in every fibre of her, a longing for him making her faint and almost feverish. It drowned out everything else.

He looked up critically and saw her, holding her gaze until a slow flush of colour flooded her skin. The silence hung between them like a curtain, desire like glittering stars flashing in the air, and he put his brush down with a slow, almost absent-minded movement, walking across like a sleep-walker to stand and look down at her.

She was not able to turn away this time. She didn't even want to, and his face was strained and white, his eyes lost in hers. He ran his hand over her throat, moving downwards, his open palm brushing erotically across her swollen breast.

'Now, Emma! Oh, dear God, now!' he sighed.

He scooped her up, a shudder running through him at her instant submission, and he walked from the studio as she lay curled in his arms, no fear in her at all, just an aching desire to own Jake as he wanted to own her.

He walked into her bedroom, kicking the door closed, pausing only to turn the key and then moving to place her on the bed and look down at her. It was only for a short, quivering second, though. He came down beside her, turning her towards him, his hands running feverishly over her skin.

'How long have I wanted you?' he asked thickly. 'I think it must have been all my life!'

He parted her lips, searching her mouth hungrily, gathering her tightly against him when she melted at once and wound her arms around his neck. His hands moved almost angrily to toss aside the robe, grasping her eagerly again when she rolled away and struggled out of it.

'Emma, Emma! Don't leave me this time or it's going to be the end of me altogether. Let me have you now!'

He groaned against her skin but she had no thought of leaving him. Her nightmare was gone, lost in the need to be close to Jake, lost in the desire that had grown as she had watched him.

She murmured against his lips, her hands restless against his shirt, pleasure racing through her as he tore it over his head and drew her to the power of his chest, her delicate skin shivering against the rasp of black masculine hair that tingled against her breasts.

'How long ago is it since I tasted you?' He nuzzled against her neck, moving beneath the silk of her hair. 'Did you really believe I wanted that girl I was painting? My eyes watched her, my fingers painted her likeness, but my mind never left my tantalising prisoner. My imagination followed you from room to room, watched you, wanted you.'

If he had wanted to drive her to desperation he could not have done more than he was doing then. His lips traced each inch of her skin like fire, his fingers caressing the swollen mounds of her breasts, recognising the desire that raged inside her.

'You're beautiful, perfect,' he breathed, 'soft and innocent as a pale rose.'

He moved downwards over her, kissing the slender length of her body, his hand tenderly caressing the thin white scar on the inside of her knee, and for a minute it shocked her. He felt her slight withdrawal and looked up at her with dark, fevered eyes.

'You think it bothers me?' he whispered huskily. 'Sometimes I want it to stay. Sometimes I never want you to get better from it. I know it's selfish, typical of me altogether, but I don't want you to be able to dance away from me. I want you defenceless, vulnerable, utterly in need of me—*mine*!'

It didn't make her feel defenceless, oddly enough. It made her feel as if she had a power over him. Her fingers reached out and brushed the dark hair that had fallen across his forehead, and his eyes darkened even more. He turned his face against her, his hand gentle against her knee, his lips moving higher against the inside of her thigh. There was a bright triumph in his eyes as he looked up at her when she gasped and clenched her hands against his smooth shoulder, her body beginning to toss restlessly.

'Wait for me.' He rolled smoothly to his feet and undressed, coming back to her and gathering her in his arms before the power of him could scare her at all. For minutes his eyes roamed over her, the pale silk of her skin increasing the urgency in him.

He clasped her close, moulding her to the length of him, his mouth covering hers in a kiss that had no end, and she clung to him, kissing him hungrily, no awareness in her of anything but Jake and the aching feeling that raced over her as she moved against him, glorying in the hard strength of his body, all fear gone as she whispered his name with a far-off desperation.

'Jake! Please, Jake!'

She wasn't even aware that she was begging to be loved, but he spun her round, crushing her beneath him, his body attuned to the ripples of excitement that flared through her. His lips burned her, their mouths clinging as if they could never part as his feverish caresses dissolved her into velvet submission.

He seemed to know exactly the moment when she rode the crest of desire, his mouth cutting off her wild cry of pain and pleasure as he possessed her, and then she was swept into another world, a wondrous world of light and colour, a world she didn't want to leave, a world where Jake's arms held her fast. There was a desperation in the way they came together, Jake's power almost ferocious as she clung to him, gasping his name.

She only knew how much she had not wanted to leave that world when she came back to earth to hear her own voice demanding to stay there and opened her eyes to see Jake looking down at her with gleaming eyes, a flare of heat still colouring his cheekbones.

'Jake! I didn't want...'

'I know, I know,' he murmured against her lips. 'I didn't want to come back either. I'm glad I did, though, because now I can see you again, now I know it's real. We'll go back there again, Emma, many, many times. I won't let you go.'

He didn't let her go then. He had no desire to get up and go anywhere, and neither had she. She lay in his arms, his hands caressing her. The things they talked about were small, nonsensical, their laughter secret and soft, and Jake never let her out of his embrace, his desire for her sweeping her back more than once into the world of delight he had led her to that morning.

Emma sighed and turned her head against the tousled covers, her eyes running over the white room and the sunlight behind the gauzy curtains. Jake's room! He had said it was his. She turned back to face him.

'Jake where have you been sleeping?'

'Away from you,' he growled, tightening her to him. 'There's a small, lonely room close to the studio,' he added with a quick smile. 'You want to see it?'

'When you lived here—before—did you...?'

His hand cupped her face, making her meet his eyes.

'You're sleeping in my bed,' he said softly. 'You're the first woman who has ever slept here.' He looked at her steadily. 'It doesn't mean there have been no women in my life, Emma. I'm not a boy. Not one of them has ever been in this room, though, I swear it. If they had I could never have brought you here. You're special, different, wonderful!'

He had never spoken like that before, so deeply, and she gazed back at him silently. Everything inside her recognised what Jake meant to her. It was like seeing her own life force, acknowledging the despair there would be without him.

Tears sprang into her eyes and she brushed them away impatiently.

'Emma,' he said urgently. 'I can't go back and wipe out my past.'

'I—I wouldn't want you to,' she managed to say, her smile growing over the tears. 'I—I'm just dreading being away from you.'

'You're not going to be,' he ground out fiercely, pulling her tightly into his arms again. 'I won't even let you think about it; I won't let you out of my sight!'

Over the next few weeks it seemed that he never would. He finished the picture and it was beautiful, not something she would have ever wanted anyone to see. Not that it was in any way erotic. It was a delicate description of her soul. That was the only way she could describe it, and Jake looked at it for a long time and then covered it.

'It's for the farm when the place is finished,' he said quietly.

'When I'm not there, will you look at it?' she asked a little wistfully. He had never mentioned permanence except for impassioned words when he made love to her. His reaction made her gasp. He jerked her forward, hard against his chest.

'What do you mean, when you're not there? You'll be there.' His dark eyes blazed into hers. 'If you leave me, Emma...!'

'I wouldn't know how,' she whispered, her hand gentle against his aggressive face.

'You'll never get the chance.' He held her close, his tight frame slowly relaxing. 'I'll never let you go more than a few steps from me.'

Of course, he had to let her out of his sight. There were commissions that had piled up while he had been in England, and Emma was left waiting for him many times as he discussed work with other people. One morning she suddenly realised she had missed her appointment at the hospital, almost two months ago, and guilt showed on her face as she told Jake.

'I never even had the courtesy to write and explain,' she said in a horrified voice.

'So many things shock you, sweetheart,' he laughed, turning to look at her as he fastened his tie. 'Skelton will have crossed you off his books as one of the best things in life. Wonder who he's admiring now?' he added thoughtfully, turning back to the mirror.

'Jake! This is serious!' She bit her lip and paced about. 'I ought to see him. I should be much further forward now with this leg.'

'Do you want to be?' He came across and locked his arms around her waist, looking down at her. 'You know how I feel.'

'I want to be normal, Jake. I want to be able to keep pace with you, dance with you.'

He watched her moodily for a few minutes and then nodded, his lips brushing hers.

'All right. You stay here this morning and write your excuses. Make an appointment privately and I'll take you back to see him.'

'Oh, Jake! Will you?' She gazed up at him adoringly and he tightened her against him.

'It's what you want, so naturally you're going to go back to see him. In any case,' he added softly, 'I want to take you back because I've got a surprise to spring on you. Two surprises, actually.'

'Oh, tell me, Jake!' She was delighted, but he laughed down at her, shaking his head.

'Just tell me one of them, then?' she wheedled.

He refused, but it left her smiling as he always left her smiling now, especially when he looked at her like that, as if he loved her.

It was hard to write the letter because she couldn't think of any excuse at all. Everything she thought of was a lie. Finally she just said that she was living in Italy and could she come back to see him privately as she was coming for a brief visit home? She had to leave it at that.

She was just going to take the letter down for Enrico to post when she heard footsteps on the marble stairs, Antonia's and someone else's. It certainly wasn't Jake, and she looked up in surprise when with a knock Antonia stood there, looking very dismayed, a tall blonde just behind her.

'A visitor, *signorina*,' she said with difficulty, struggling with the language. 'It is for Signor Garrani, but he is out and she did not wish to wait.'

'I don't think you would have wanted me to wait, would you?'

The woman simply pushed her way into the room and shut the door in Antonia's annoyed face. It was then, in the light, that Emma knew where she had seen her before. She was the woman in the picture Jake had sold, the picture he had told her he wanted to be rid of. *Ecstasy*. She looked harder, cold, older, but it was the same woman, Emma had not one doubt, and she remembered too that Jake had told her he was on the run when she had first burst into his life. On the run from this woman?

A tight, heavy feeling grew inside, her confidence drained, and the woman seemed to know at once. She came in as if she knew the room, as if she had been here many times before.

'I can see this isn't a single room. It never was, mind you. I was here myself for long enough, as that wretched woman downstairs remembers well. She never liked me. If she could have kept me out she would have done.'

Emma's face tightened at the thought of Antonia being pushed about.

'If you've come to see Jake then you already know he's out. If you want to wait the normal thing to do is to be shown into a downstairs reception-room. It's not really normal to push your way into the bedroom.'

'It is if it's my husband's bedroom. Perhaps I should have introduced myself? I'm Linda Garrani, Jake's wife, and you, I take it, are his latest love-affair?'

Icy cold fingers seemed to trail across Emma's skin. She stared at the woman, at the beautiful face.

'It's not true! Not Jake! He wouldn't...!'

'He would and has frequently.' Linda Garrani walked impatiently to the window and looked out. 'That damned courtyard! I always hated it here.' She spun round. 'If you don't believe me, ask Antonia, ask Enrico.' She smiled bitterly. 'Better still, ask Jake.'

Emma didn't need to. She had sufficient common sense to know that nobody would have been able to force their way into this house if they hadn't been genuine. Antonia might dislike this woman but she had let her in; she had got past Enrico, and that took some doing.

'What do you want?' she asked in a dull voice.

'What do I *want*? My dear, you've got to be unreal to ask that! Jake is my husband! Maybe you should have asked where I've been? A series of love-affairs is not something that's easy to take, although I'll give you one boost to your morale—he doesn't usually bring them here. You must be something special.'

Emma watched her without really seeing her any more. There was no sign of hesitation in the bored and angry voice. It was all too real.

'I left Jake, and not for the first time. I always come back, though.' She gave a sharp bitter laugh. 'I've never found a mistress actually installed in the house before.'

Everything inside Emma was crying out that it couldn't be true, but every look that crossed Linda Garrani's face told her it was. So many of Jake's remarks now made sense, little things he had said. He had told her he would never let her leave him, but he had never mentioned marriage. How could he when he was already married? He was as much married as Gareth had been.

What would he say when he came back? How could she face him? She knew without too much delving into her own character that she could not. If he simply acknowledged this and shrugged in that indifferent way he had it would kill her. And if he refused to let her go...

She sat on the bed and then jumped up, her mind wanting to escape from the memories of the love she had felt in this room. She moved as far away as possible, and Linda Garrani's eyes followed her movements.

'You're lame?' she noted quietly. 'A crushed sparrow! Damn Jake! It would be his idea of new excitement.'

There was disgust and pity in the voice now, and it convinced Emma more than anything else could have done. Jake didn't want her to be better. He wanted her to be defenceless and vulnerable—his! The words swept through her mind and she turned to the other woman, her face pale.

'Can you prove you're Jake's wife?' She knew she was hanging on to the last threads of happiness, but even they were dashed.

'It's something I've been asked before, plenty of times,' Linda Garrani said with a pitying look at Emma. 'They never believe it, my dear. Jake is the very devil at convincing people.'

She opened her bag and Emma could not pretend any more. It was a copy of a marriage certificate. Jake's marriage certificate.

'You may think it odd that I carry it about, but I'm never believed when I have to rescue Jake's conquests and get them clear of him. It's easier to simply leave it in my bag.'

'If I'm leaving it's got to be before Jake comes back. He'll never let me go.' Emma's face was completely white, and the older woman looked at her sympathetically.

'He will, my dear. He'll tire of you, limp and all.' She stood with a resigned air about her. 'I'll get you out of here, but you'd better move fast. If you can pack quickly I'll get you to the plane and away. Have you got any money?'

'Yes, I have.'

'Well, that makes a nice change—normally they borrow from me.'

It cut into Emma even worse. She had drawn out her money in England, kept it by her. Had her instincts even then told her what to expect? The words too made her feel sick deep inside—'normally they borrow from me'.

How many times? How many girls had gone away with Jake and been humiliated like this?

'I'll pack,' she said numbly.

She thought at first that Enrico would try to stop her. He was in the hall with Antonia, anger on his face as he watched them come down the stairs.

'*Signorina*! You cannot go away. I am supposed to care for you when Signor Garrani is not here. This woman——!'

Linda Garrani interrupted, speaking in Italian, a vicious flow of words that silenced him, and then they were walking away, getting into the car that had been waiting in the street, and Emma dared not turn round for even one last look at the house. She feared that if she did nothing would be able to prevent her from going back to Jake.

It was only when she had landed in London that the desolation really began to hit her. She had done what she had always done, crushed the feeling, hidden it inside. This time, though, it would not sink into the far reaches of her mind. It was out in the open, surging up, despair shaking her whole body, her mind crying Jake's name and refusing to stop.

To stay in London was out of the question. To go back to Devon was also not possible. She could never again face a house where Jake had been—his memory would stalk the rooms—and London was too expensive. She got a room for one night at a cheap hotel, locked the door and settled down to think, forcing away the thought of Jake every time his image rose in her mind. There was one thing about a big city; it was utterly impersonal, uncaring. It was possible to be alone here, even when crowds walked by.

She would have to get some sort of job and pull her life together. She was only half trained, but she did have some useful skills. She went out and bought the papers and began to look. It kept her mind away from Jake. There would only be the nights when he could come back and haunt her.

It was funny, Emma mused; she wasn't afraid of anything any more. Without Jake nothing seemed to matter. Things that would normally have thrown her into a panic simply washed right over her. It was a matter of getting the priorities right, and the priority now was simply to survive without him. The time would come perhaps when she would even be able to read his name and feel nothing but anger, but it was too soon.

She tried for a job at a private nursing home for old people. It was a cheerful-looking place and surrounded by gardens, even though it was well into the city. Before Jake had come into her life she would have been nervous, but now she had the confidence that came from not really caring what people thought.

The matron was a pleasant, kind-looking woman and she was interested in the fact that Emma was a partly trained physiotherapist.

'We have a man who comes once a week to ease their aches and pains, but sometimes they could do with quick help. It may be possible for you to work with him and advance your training. Why did you stop?'

'I had an accident,' Emma said truthfully, meeting her eyes. 'You've probably noticed that I walk with a slight limp?'

'Well, I did, but unless it bothers you too much I can't see that it's going to hinder you here. Everything's on one level for the old people. There would only be stairs when you went to your room.'

'Would I live in?' It was a godsend. It would solve all her problems at one go, a job and living accommodation.

'Oh, yes. We would certainly want that.'

'It suits me,' Emma said. 'I'll be glad to live here.'

It had all been so easy. She was needed at once and she could hardly believe her good fortune. Day by day, a step at a time, she would have to learn to live without Jake, and here she would be busy seeing to other people's problems. Surely her own would fade? In any case, she had to get on with her life because she knew she would never see Jake again.

CHAPTER TEN

EMMA settled in at the end of the week, her room a small, cosy place. She was one of several people working and living in, but it was not possible yet to lower her guard sufficiently to be friendly. She was still too raw. She had walked into Jake's life and then walked out of it, but the time there with him had been her greatest happiness. He had taught her to live. Now she had to begin again without him.

It took three weeks to get an appointment with Mr Skelton, his list was so full, and he gave her his usual searching look. If he now saw no sign of the glow on her face he said nothing, and her leg was no worse, at least.

When she went to make her next appointment there was a great long queue at the appointment clerk's desk, and the woman there met Emma's eyes ruefully.

'Give me your card and I'll call you when your turn comes up,' she suggested, and Emma wandered away to the waiting area close by, her fingers idly flicking through the magazines, her ears attuned for her name being called.

She wondered which consultant's wife took this glossy gossip magazine. It seemed a funny place to find it. She looked at the pictures and the sharp comments below some of them. She wasn't really interested in who had flown out and in, who had been to which ball.

And suddenly Jake's face was staring up at her from the page, scowling, his black brows drawn together in a fury, the words below written with the usual pithy style that marked the other comments.

Jake Garrani flew in from New York last night, by some strange quirk of fortune aboard the same flight as his ex-wife Linda. It would seem that five years of being divorced has not softened his attitude towards her. Needless to say, they did not sit together!

Emma looked dazedly at the rather smug face of the woman in another photograph, a woman who was obviously leaving the same flight but who was certainly not with Jake, a woman who had convinced her of Jake's treachery. Her eyes hardly dared to look at the date. Like many magazines in waiting-rooms, it was over a year old. Jake was not married. He had divorced that woman more than six years ago. She just sat and stared at the page, her eyes seeing nothing at all.

'Miss Shaw! Miss Shaw!'

It dawned on her that she was being called, and she looked vaguely across at the desk.

'It's your turn now.' The woman came round the desk and walked towards her. 'Are you all right? Shall I get Mr Skelton's nurse?'

'No. No I—I'm fine.' Fine! She had ruined her own life! She had allowed some strange woman she had never seen before to wipe out all there was between Jake and herself. Even if she raced around, trying to find him, even if she flew back out to Florence, he would never want to see her. He had asked her to trust him and when the cards were finally down she had not trusted him at all. She stood numbly and listened to the clerk, and then took her card and walked out without having heard anything at all.

Derek Murray stood back and watched Emma work, his small comments mostly praise. She was used to working with him now, her skills returning. She could talk to people and enjoy seeing the pain ease from their faces as she worked.

'She's good, isn't she, Mr Murray?' Mrs Jameson asked, cringing a little as Emma's fingers dug into her shoulder. 'It's not nice at the time, but later it's bliss.'

'She's a lucky find, Mrs Jameson,' he answered. 'I'll be redundant soon.'

Emma gave him a smile and went on with her work. The old people here were lovely to work with and she now knew all of them, all their little problems and worries. Derek Murray had helped her a lot over the past two months, and she was beginning to immerse herself more and more into the work here. Nearly three months away from Jake and she was still functioning, learning to live without him. It was only at night and when she was alone that Jake's image came forward, his dark face filling her mind, her skin aching for his touch.

'You should get back to your training, Emma,' Derek Murray said as they walked along the corridor together later. 'Get your qualifications and join my practice.'

'Later I'd like to do that, but not yet,' Emma said softly. 'Right now I'm happy here.'

'That's a lie if ever I heard one,' he commented, reaching for his coat. 'I think you're hiding here. Your brisk image slips sometimes. I think somebody hurt you badly.'

She looked up at him and shook her head.

'He didn't. I hurt myself. I just had no trust.'

He looked at her for a second and then shook his head.

'Go back. I can't understand an attitude like that.'

'There's no going back.'

There was no going back, not with Jake. She had deserted him, not trusted him, made him look a fool in front of Enrico and Antonia. She had come down on the side of a stranger. No, there was no going back. She was building a life without him, slowly, it was true, but each day she tried and it was working.

When she was off duty she settled in her room for the evening, had a bath and switched on the television. She had everything done for her here. All her meals were prepared, her room cleaned. She was almost like a patient herself. She did her evening exercises and looked down at her leg. The small scar was almost invisible now and there was definite ease of movement.

Derek Murray had been telling her about one of his patients who had been involved in a similar accident. It had taken three years and he still had a limp, but they were certain he would get better completely. Mr Skelton had told her the same thing. He had also told her that another operation might do the trick. It was something she would have to consider. It might be worth the pain and the slight risk, but at the moment she was coping well.

She made herself a cup of tea and sat down again, her eyes now on the pictures on the small screen. It was her long weekend, the time when she had to fight Jake away as if he were really there. But she was almost asleep when a voice she knew so well had her sitting bolt upright, her eyes wide open. Jake!

He was there, right in front of her on television. He was sitting comfortably, talking to the chat-show host who had celebrities on twice a week. She stumbled forward and turned up the sound, Jake's voice filling her ears, the sight of him bringing tears into her eyes.

'No,' he was saying, 'I'm not having a show at all. One was partly planned but I cancelled it. I have something more important to do.'

Her eyes feasted on him, running over his face, watching those beautiful, clever hands that had brought her such wild joy. His hair needed cutting and he was wearing a black denim shirt again, his brown throat powerful and strong. What was he doing here in England? Did he think of her? Who was with him now?

She found she was saying his name over and over again, almost missing the words of the interviewer.

'You were telling me, Jake, that you've done your best ever portrait. Is this the one?'

'Yes. This is it. If I never paint again it will all have been worthwhile for this one. I'll never do better.'

'Can we see it?'

Jake leaned over and uncovered a framed picture, the camera panning in to get a good shot, and Emma saw her own face looking back at her, her grey-blue dress painted as if it were real, the red scarf bright against it. But there were no buttons unfastened, no knee showing, and even if there had been the face would have held all eyes away from such things. It was soft and bewildered, almost dazed with the astonished realisation of love, everything that had grown as Jake had painted her, everything he had not let her see.

Jake had seen, though. Jake had known she loved him, and his small tricks with buttons and skirt had been to lead her into the trust she had then cast aside. He had refused to let her see it so that she would not know. It would have frightened her and he knew it.

'Oh, Jake!' She sat and whispered his name as the cameras drew back and Jake's face came into view.

'You usually name your work. Does this have a name?'

'It has a name,' Jake said deeply. 'The name of the girl who modelled for it. She came into my life out of nowhere and then went back to nowhere. The portrait is *Emma*.'

He looked up at the camera and seemed to be looking right into her eyes.

'Emma!' He said it again, so low, so softly that tears swam in her eyes, allowing her to see nothing else. The credits were rolling down the screen before she moved, her eyes frantically dried as she waited for the channel sign.

She stumbled down to the office, feverishly dialling the studio, desperate to catch him. In her heart she knew he wanted to see her, even if it was just once more, and she wanted to see him, to hear his voice, even if he raged at her.

She didn't know who answered. She had no idea who to ask for because her mind wasn't working at all.

'I have to speak to Mr Garrani. I have to catch him before he leaves the studio!'

'Mr Garrani? One moment, please.'

There was silence, nothing, and then the well-modulated voice was back on the line.

'I'm sorry, madam, but the programme you've just been watching was recorded. It was recorded two weeks ago.'

'But I must speak to him! You must know where he is! How did you get in touch with him in the first place? You've got to help me. *Please*!'

Her frantic words did nothing to unsettle the calm of the voice. Maybe they were used to lunatics ringing?

'If you could hold the line, madam.'

It seemed like hours but it could only have been minutes, after all, before the line was once again alive.

'I've spoken to the producer,' the voice said as if this was quite extraordinary and a thing not to be repeated. 'We're not allowed to give out the addresses of the people who come on television, but the producer said that if you could give your number he is able to get in touch with Mr Garrani. If I could have your number now?'

Emma read out the number of the office phone, saying it twice, certain that something would go wrong.

'And your name, madam?'

'Emma. Just tell him it's Emma.'

She had no idea how that went down, but it was all that was necessary. If Jake wanted to see her he would not need another name. Her hands were trembling and she sat down, staring at the telephone. She was in her dressing-gown, but she didn't care who saw her. Nothing would get her away from this phone. If anyone came and ordered her out of the office it would take three strong men to move her. Jake was somewhere in London. He had to be, and he hated things like television chat shows. He must want to see her, he must!

When the phone rang she snatched it up, and Jake's voice was at the other end of the line.

'Emma?'

For a moment she couldn't answer, the wild beating of her own heart choking her.

'Emma? Emma, please answer me!'

'Jake! Oh, Jake . . .' Her voice trailed away into tears, and he spoke quickly, his voice low and urgent.

'Don't put the phone down. Tell me where you are. Keep talking to me, Emma. Where are you?'

He sounded desperate, and she wiped at her eyes with shaking fingers, managing to give him the address.

'Jake . . . !'

'No! Don't talk to me. Just stay there. Don't move. I'll be there in minutes. Promise me you'll be there!'

'I'll be here, Jake,' she whispered.

Long before he arrived she was downstairs, waiting on the step, her eyes straining into the darkness for signs of a car coming up the drive, her heart beating so much that she could hear nothing else.

She knew it was Jake before the car turned into the drive. It was coming so fast along the road that he had to brake sharply to make the bend. The headlights flared over her, the car stopped, and then he was out, standing beside her, his face pale even in the lights of the doorway. She wanted to throw herself into his arms but she wouldn't have dared, and Jake showed no sign of reaching for her.

'Can you just walk away?' His eyes moved over the building and then back to her.

'It's my long weekend. I don't have to be back until Tuesday.'

He just nodded curtly and took her arm, hurrying her into the car, turning it quickly and driving fast. It was only when they were well down the road that he allowed the car to maintain a more reasonable speed. At least they wouldn't end up in a police cell for the night, but Emma wouldn't have minded if they did. She was close to Jake, next to him, her eyes moving over the harsh profile that was resolutely staring ahead. She knew he was angry but he had wanted to see her. It was all that mattered.

'Jake——' she began softly, but he stopped her at once.

'No! If you're going to tell me you're sorry then I don't want to know. If you want explanations then they'll have to wait.'

The raw sound of his voice made her skin shiver, and she longed to touch him but she knew better. The old rage was inside him, the black brows scowling, and she wondered again if he had merely wanted to see her to rage at her. He was not the sort of man to accept the way she had behaved.

It was the same old street where he stopped, the same people hanging around talking, and the talking stopped as he drew up and got out. For once they were not calling out to him, not wanting to show off their latest work, and he didn't look as if he would have welcomed any interruptions. His tight face made her heart thump, and she had no idea what he was going to say. After her unforgivable action she could hardly expect a man like Jake to forgive.

He moved her inside the flat and closed the door on the interested onlookers, switching on the lights, making Emma blink in the sudden brightness. It was so cosy, so familiar, the curtains drawn against the night, and she looked up anxiously as Jake stood watching her.

His dark eyes looked into hers, his gaze moving over her, and she could only stand there, trembling, waiting for the anger. It was wonderful to just see him again, and she was aware of nothing but Jake, her gaze hungry on his face.

And suddenly he smiled, the dark eyes softened, the dark, restless face filled with joy.

'Emma, *love*!'

He opened his arms and she just walked into them, her own arms winding around his neck as he crushed her close.

Wave after wave of joy raced over her as Jake held her close. She knew he had wanted to find her and she hoped for a miracle, but deep inside she had dreaded his anger. This tender loving when he should have been blaming her for her lack of trust left her bewildered.

'Jake?' She lifted her head and tried to look up at him, to begin to explain, but he was still content to hold her, not willing to let her even step away and talk.

'No, no! Later, darling,' he whispered, his hand cupping her face, his lips no more than a mere breath away from her own. 'Emma, Emma! How have you been, my little love? How did you manage?'

His lips moved feverishly over her face, his hand in her hair as she lifted her face to be kissed.

'I couldn't find you,' he groaned, his lips against her mouth. 'You didn't go back to Eric's and I knew you had nowhere to go but there. I didn't know if you had any money, anywhere to sleep... Oh, darling, I've been so scared for you! How did you manage without me?'

'I—I got a job, Jake. I thought I'd never see you again.'

Tears came into her eyes but they were happy tears now, and he knew it. He held her away from him and looked at her intently, his dark eyes devouring her, anxiety still deep in his gaze.

'Let me look at you. Let me be quite sure you're here.' His eyes followed the slender lines of her body and then raised to hers, a blaze of love so clear that her own eyes closed as he drew her back to safety and warmth.

All the black despair flew as if it had never been, and her arms moved tightly around him, clinging and never letting go. It was only when her legs trembled and her lips were burning that he let her go, and then only to take her to the white settee and sit down with her gathered close to him.

'I found you,' he murmured against her hair. 'I was beginning to think I never would. I was beginning to think you were going to hide from me for the rest of your life. I came on the next flight and I've been looking for you ever since.' He looked down into her eyes, his hand warm against her face. 'Tell me you'll never, ever leave me again,' he demanded fiercely.

'I never will. I didn't want to then, but Linda said——'

'For God's sake, don't call her that! Don't give her a name,' he said angrily. He suddenly went quiet and looked down at her, holding her away. 'Do you still think I'm married?'

'No.' Emma shook her head. 'I saw a magazine, an old one. You were in it and so was she. It said you were divorced and had been for five years.' She looked up, sorrow on her face. 'Oh, Jake! How can I tell you I'm sorry? How can I when I didn't trust you enough to stay and face you?'

'Did my life hang on the chance of your looking through an old magazine?' he asked deeply. 'Suppose you'd never seen it? Suppose all you'd seen was the broadcast? Would you have got in touch with me?'

'Yes.' She looked at him steadily, her blue eyes serious. 'I couldn't have seen you again and not tried to be with you. Even if... I love you,' she said a little desperately. 'I couldn't have stayed away when I knew you were looking for me.'

'You don't have to apologise to me for loving me,' he said softly, a smile deep in his eyes. 'How did you know I was looking for you?'

'I saw you and I saw the picture. I understood a lot more then. You seemed to be looking straight at me, as if you wanted me to call you.'

'It was like praying in public,' he growled, his arms tightening. 'I know that particular producer. He's been trying to get me to do an interview for about four years, but that's not really my style. First of all I went round every hospital to see if you were training again. Then I came here and locked myself in to think. It occurred to me that you might be in some private practice, so I got a good deal of help. Almost everyone on this street has been doing the rounds, knocking on doors, asking about you. We've pestered every physiotherapist and private clinic in London.'

'Oh, Jake!' She could suddenly see him doing it, his grim determination. It made her laugh and he scowled at her ferociously.

'You little nuisance,' he growled. 'How was I expected to find you? I called in the only army I had.'

She wound her arms around his neck, covering his face with wild little kisses, but he held her away and looked down at her with darkening eyes.

'Not yet,' he begged in a shaken voice. 'I want to get everything out of the way first. Later you can have all the love you want—more than you can take, the way I feel.'

He folded her close and went on talking.

'We turned up nothing, not one clue,' he said in a harrassed voice. 'The television appearance was my last idea. I made it on the understanding that if you rang he would get to me at once, and then I just sat and waited— for two whole weeks longer! I must have paced a worn patch in this carpet, day and night. Even then, I didn't know if you would see it, or even if you did I didn't know if you'd have enough faith in me to come.'

'She was so convincing, Jake,' Emma said quietly. 'I suppose I never could believe that someone like you would really want me with you...'

Her voice trailed away and she bit into her lower lip. He had never said that even this time was permanent.

'That someone like me would want you forever?' he asked quietly, turning her face where he could see it. 'It was forever very soon after I first saw you, darling. I had to work out how I was going to get you cured of all that fright, though. I couldn't marry you and live nicely and comfortably as your friend. I wanted to take care of you, cherish you, but I wanted you too. In Florence all my hopes came true.'

His lips closed warmly over hers and he crushed her against him for breathless minutes.

'Can you remember that I said I'd bring you to England and that I had two surprises for you?'

Emma looked up at him and nodded, too filled with joy to speak.

'One was the portrait of you. It was going to be the centre-piece of my latest show, the best thing I've ever done in my life. The other surprise was a wedding, yours and mine.'

'And I didn't trust you.' Tears filled Emma's eyes and he grasped her chin, forcing her to look at him.

'No guilt,' he ordered sternly. 'You've lived long enough with guilt, fear and pain. I should have behaved like any normal person and told you about my ex-wife. I had to be sure you were cured before I asked you to marry me, Emma,' he explained urgently. 'I knew I couldn't stay with you every day of my life and not touch you. Making love is part of loving, the final expression of it, the thing that makes two people into one, and I love you so damned much. I should have asked you to marry me right away instead of behaving like a sultan with a captive.'

It brought a smile to Emma's lips, a smile that was reflected in his eyes, and she sat up straight, her soft lips determined.

'You can tell me about your ex-wife now,' she ordered, looking at him firmly when exasperation crossed his dark face.

'I could explode just thinking about her!' he grated. 'I suppose I'd better tell you, but it's going to be quick. After this I can do without any word of her.'

Emma nodded and waited, her face telling him that she intended to hear it right now.

'All right.' He grinned and held her close. 'I've got a place in New York. I used to be there a lot. I like it there. That's where I met Linda, at a party. She came to pose for me and she was very glamorous.' He looked at Emma ruefully. 'Like many men, I thought that was what I wanted. Linda's beauty is exceptionally skin-deep,' he continued drily. 'Right from the word go we were like enemies. She had her life mapped out like a military operation, and I was just one small part of it. She wanted parties, travel and money. I seemed to be a good idea and nothing more. Life was one long fight and I hated every minute of it; almost from the first I knew it couldn't last.

'I was away a lot, and I was working hard. Linda still kept up the parties, and the rumours I heard proved not to be rumours after a while. She had someone else and I wanted a divorce.' He moved irritably, clearly wanting to say nothing more, but Emma waited and he went on after a second.

'Linda didn't want a divorce. She was quite content to have her cake and eat it too. The whole thing was pretty messy. I had to fight my way clear. By then I was doing very well indeed, and she wanted to hang on. It was a long-drawn-out battle. After that she did her best to haunt me. She turned up wherever I happened to be, her whole purpose to cause trouble. I was supposed to be embarrassed. I was simply enraged. That was when I sold the portrait of her, and I suppose I did it out of sheer meanness. She never did want anyone to see that. I then took off to Devon with the intention of staying there a whole year and hoping she'd tire of following me around. I never wanted to see a woman again.' He shrugged. 'End of story, except that one foggy evening a wisp of a girl with deep blue eyes and a haunted look came crashing into my life and taught me to really love.'

Emma lay quietly in his arms, and after a minute he turned her face to his, anxiety in his glance.

'Do you mind very much, sweetheart?' he asked softly. 'Does she bother you?'

'Linda? No. I should have known it was all a lie. Enrico tried to stop me from going, but I wouldn't listen to him—at least, I might have done, but Linda interrupted and she spoke Italian. I don't even know what she said.'

'Yes, she speaks Italian—her mother was Italian. She said you wanted to go and she was rescuing you,' Jake muttered ferociously. 'She told him you'd had enough of being trapped there.'

'Oh, Jake!' Emma looked at him with shock and anger in her eyes.

'Luckily I didn't believe a word of it,' he murmured, his eyes smiling. 'I had that portrait and I can read expressions. I knew that a sweet, gentle girl loved me against all odds. I knew you wanted me. I also knew that Linda had used some very convincing story and I guessed she'd told you I was still married to her.'

'She said she used to live there with you and that it had been her bedroom too,' Emma said in a low voice. 'She said it wasn't the first time she had rescued your—your victims.'

It didn't bring on any sort of rage. He gave a short bark of laughter.

'She never lived there. She came there and made a scene on two occasions—that's how Enrico and Antonia knew her. She never got up those stairs, however. As to the other, the women in my life were before I got married at all,' he assured her. 'Even then they were few and far between. After Linda I swore there would be no other woman at all. I began to dislike the gender.'

'Oh! No wonder you disliked me when I met you in the fog,' Emma commented. 'You were absolutely horrid. You scared me.'

'Not as much as you scared me,' Jake informed her deeply. 'You had me in the greatest fix I've ever been in my whole life. Almost at once I knew you were terrified of men, scared to be touched, and almost at once too I knew I wanted you as I've never wanted any woman before. I couldn't even plan any sort of strategy to get you. I had to take each day as it came and you drove me wild, wandering off into the fog, refusing to talk about your problems. At the party I knew you wanted me almost as much as I wanted you, but straight after that you were back behind your barrier, locking me out. When that Gareth person arrived I wanted to kill him.'

'I used to feel fairly safe with him, Jake,' Emma explained. 'I thought—thought I might be able to be normal with Gareth. When he told me he was married I imagined I was heartbroken, but then there was you, and finally you were going to Italy, going to leave me.'

'I had to drive you out into the open,' he murmured with even now a sort of desperation. 'I had to make you step towards me and leave at least some of your fears behind. Then I had to make you jealous, and after that I had to...'

'Make me want you too much to wait,' Emma finished for him.

'Are you sorry?'

His hands moved over her slowly, the first time he had shown any desire, the first time since they had come in that he had allowed his feelings to take any control at all.

'No. Even when I thought you were married, I wasn't sorry about that. I was happier then than I've ever been. Will you take me back there, Jake?'

'Try and stop me.'

His hand moved under her soft sweater, searching for the warm excitement of her skin, his eyes locked with hers until she closed her own eyes and surrendered to the waves of pleasure that his caresses brought.

'Do you remember that store-room with all the paint and canvases?' Emma asked in a trembling voice.

'I'll never forget it,' Jake said thickly. 'It's better here, though. When you stayed here before, you slept in my bed for the first time and I could have stayed there all night, watching you. Tonight I'm going to.'

He lifted her up and carried her through to the bedroom, his hands warm and tender as he undressed her.

'Will you marry me, darling?' he asked huskily as she lay in his arms.

'Tomorrow?' Emma wanted to know, her smile secret and thrilled.

He shook his dark head, his face already taut with desire.

'I can't let you out of my arms so soon,' he murmured against her lips. 'The day after—we'll give it some thought.'

His mouth closed over hers and she was swept into the delight that only Jake could bring, his tenderness finally lost in a feverish desire to hold her close and own her again after so long.

'What about your leg?' he asked afterwards when she lay dreamily in his arms. 'Did you see Skelton?'

'Yes. It's getting better and I have a choice. I can have another operation or wait for the whole thing to get better by itself.'

'Will it?' Jake asked, turning her flushed face to his, his eyes searching her expression.

'Perhaps,' she said steadily. 'It may take a long time, though. Derek says that...'

'Who the hell is Derek?' He came up on one elbow and glared down at her.

There was a tense pressure in his fingers, his eyes punishing, and an intoxicating feeling raced through Emma to think that this dark, powerful man was tight with jealousy at even the mention of another man's name.

'He comes to the home to do the physiotherapy. I've been working with him. He's invited me to join his practice when I've finished training.'

'Indeed?' Jake said derisively. 'And where do you think you're going to finish your training? You'll be far too busy to train for anything!'

'I should have a job of some sort,' Emma murmured, delighted to be able to tease him.

For a second the black scowl came back, and then he saw the laughter in her eyes and his arms brought her close in a swift hard movement.

'You've got a job,' he assured her softly, his dark eyes on her lips. 'You're going to be the wife of Jake Garrani. Artists need a lot of looking after, so do their children. The world will have to manage without you.'

He brought the subject of her treatment up later when she lay flushed and breathless in his arms.

'What do you want to do about the leg, darling?' he asked gently. 'Whatever you decide is all right by me.'

'I might wait,' Emma told him. 'I can give it a lot longer yet. I can keep coming back to Mr Skelton and I can see what happens. It may take a long time,' she added, glancing at him.

'What am I supposed to say about that?' Jake asked softly, his hand cupping her face.

'Linda said I was a crushed sparrow,' she said, her eyes blue and wide on his face.

He lifted her into his arms, cradling her close.

'I love you,' he said deeply. 'Whatever you're like, I love you. It's not because of any lameness that I've protected you. I wanted you to keep the fragile sweetness that's inside you. I wanted to make sure that you got no more knocks in your life, no more unhappiness. Any decision is yours.'

'I'll have the operation, then,' Emma announced firmly.

Three months later, as Jake brought her home to Florence, Emma felt she could almost dance beside him. The three months had changed her enormously. Jake's love and care had wiped any lingering sadness from her eyes. The operation had been successful, and when she had come round Jake had been there, his hand holding hers, fear on his face until she had turned her head and smiled at him.

The room had been filled with flowers, a huge arrangement of red roses from Jake and so many more from the artists in the street who had joined in the search for her. They had been at the wedding too and now she was home, back in Florence with Jake, back in the house behind the secret wall, but this time Enrico and Antonia had called her Signora Garrani.

It was just the same. The cool marble hall, the staircase with the glitter of gilt, and she went eagerly from room to room, just looking at everything she had expected never to see again, her footsteps light and quick, Antonia and Enrico watching from the hall, where Jake stood smiling as she finished her happy inspection.

'The lift can go if you like.'

She came back out to smile up at Jake and his arm came round her instantly, delight on his face that she was so happy, that she was once again able to walk without pain. She heard Enrico busily translating for Antonia and saw Antonia's face looking quite shocked as she quickly appealed to Jake.

'What does she say?' Emma asked, imagining she had offended the small, bird-like woman who had greeted her so warmly.

'She begs you to reconsider—to keep the lift,' Jake explained softly, his dark eyes watching her for reaction. 'She wants me to remind you that there are a lot of stairs and she's quite sure that you must by now be having my child. At any rate, she thinks we've been married long enough.'

Emma's face flushed like a rose, and Antonia looked well pleased.

'How did she know?' Emma asked quietly, lowering her voice so that only Jake could hear.

'Wishful thinking,' Jake said firmly, and then his dark eyebrows rose, his eyes opening wide as the impact of her words hit him. 'Did you expect to keep it a secret?' he asked huskily.

'Only until we got up to our room,' she assured him, her eyes laughing into his. 'You kept two secrets for me when I was here before. I've saved a secret for you now. I didn't have another secret to give you.'

A great wave of tenderness crossed his face and he turned her to the flight of marble stairs, his arm around her, his dark head against the silky darkness of hers.

'Emma, my love!' he said softly.

Next Month's Romances

Each month you can choose from a world of variety in romance with Mills & Boon. Below are the new titles to look out for next month, why not ask either Mills & Boon Reader Service or your Newsagent to reserve you a copy of the titles you want to buy — just tick the titles you would like to order and either post to Reader Service or take it to any Newsagent and ask them to order your books.

Please save me the following titles: Please tick   √

Title	Author	
A HONEYED SEDUCTION	Diana Hamilton	
PASSIONATE POSSESSION	Penny Jordan	
MOTHER OF THE BRIDE	Carole Mortimer	
DARK ILLUSION	Patricia Wilson	
FATE OF HAPPINESS	Emma Richmond	
THE ALPHA MAN	Kay Thorpe	
HUNGARIAN RHAPSODY (This book is free with THE ALPHA MAN)	Jessica Steele	
NOTHING LESS THAN LOVE	Vanessa Grant	
LOVE'S VENDETTA	Stephanie Howard	
CALL UP THE WIND	Anne McAllister	
TOUCH OF FIRE	Joanna Neil	
TOMORROW'S HARVEST	Alison York	
THE STOLEN HEART	Amanda Browning	
NO MISTAKING LOVE	Jessica Hart	
THE BEGINNING OF THE AFFAIR	Marjorie Lewty	
CAUSE FOR LOVE	Kerry Allyne	
RAPTURE IN THE SANDS	Sandra Marton	

If you would like to order these books from Mills & Boon Reader Service please send £1.70 per title to: Mills & Boon Reader Service, P.O. Box 236, Croydon, Surrey, CR9 3RU and quote your Subscriber No:..(If applicable) and complete the name and address details below. Alternatively, these books are available from many local Newsagents including W.H.Smith, J.Menzies, Martins and other paperback stockists from 11th September 1992.

Name:..,...

Address:..

....Post Code:........................

To Retailer: If you would like to stock M&B books please contact your regular book/magazine wholesaler for details.

You may be mailed with offers from other reputable companies as a result of this application.
If you would rather not take advantage of these opportunities please tick box ☐